NOM DE PLUME

BLUEGRASS HOMECOMING - BOOK 3

JAN SCARBROUGH

SADDLE HORSE PRESS

Copyright © 2017 Jan Scarbrough
Scarbrough, Jan
Nom de Plume: Bluegrass Homecoming
Media > Books > Fiction > Romance Novels
Category/Tags: second chances, wedding

Digital ISBN: 978-0-9971920-1-8
Print ISBN 978-1-7343714-8-2

Edited by Karen Block
Cover Design by Kim Jacobs

This edition is published by agreement with Saddle Horse Press, PO Box 221543, Louisville, KY 40252.

DEDICATION

To Brenna

NOM DE PLUME

When the dream of happily-ever-after is shattered, sometimes another door opens.

Devoted homemaker and mother C.B Lyons hadn't known she was living a lie, right up until the moment when she caught her husband cheating. Betrayed and then divorced, with her dreams of a big, happy family smashed to pieces, C.B. takes her toddler son to Heritage Springs, Kentucky, to be near family. Typing manuscripts for a famous romance author seems like the perfect job until she discovers the hidden truth about the reserved, reclusive writer.

Madison Mallory is a best-selling romance author with a secret. "She" is a "he." The original Madison is actually in a nursing home. Her son, Jamie Madison, is determined she'll have the best care possible. Even if that means quitting his job and taking up his mother's pen name to keep the romance—and the money needed for her care—flowing.

Writing about romance is one thing. Making it work in real life is harder for Jamie. C.B. has good reasons to distrust men, especially sexy ones with piercing blue eyes. When C.B.'s ex wants his family back, can the author and his assistant find a way to write their own happily-ever-after ending?

CHAPTER ONE

Friday Morning
Louisville, Kentucky

"Eat your oatmeal, Scotty," Colleen Lyons said with a mother's practiced voice.

The blond-haired boy stabbed at his gooey porridge with a spoon, preferring to pound the table with the end of his utensil rather than use it for eating. Tomorrow her son turned three. It hardly seemed possible. Time had flown so fast. Colleen cast a loving glance at Scotty before she turned to the kitchen counter where the one-cup coffee maker hissed as the hazelnut brew finished flowing into a ceramic mug.

After pouring a generous amount of cream into the steaming cup of liquid, Colleen carried it to the table and placed it near her husband Daniel. He gazed at the morning paper without looking up, without acknowledging her helpfulness. That was all right. She didn't work outside the home, after all, and being a housewife and mother meant she did additional duties relieving Daniel of responsibility. He attended med school and needed time to study.

Life would be better once his schooling was complete, but that would be several years away. She could wait. Just as she waited on him daily, Colleen had patience enough for both of them. Nevertheless, she often imagined the future. It was like a shiny object just beyond her reach—Daniel in the pediatric practice with his father, Scotty going off to middle school, and maybe another child to care for, a daughter this time. She'd always wanted a big family.

Yet, there were times when Colleen bit her tongue. Like now. Daniel looked a mess. His hair was tousled and his rheumy eyes rimmed with dark circles. He remained in his pajamas—a loose-fitting Louisville Cardinals T-shirt and gray sweat pants.

She turned back to the stove where bacon sizzled. "I wish you'd drive to Heritage Springs tomorrow for Scotty's birthday party."

Using a fork to remove the bacon, Colleen drained it on a paper towel. Then she scrambled free-range eggs in a frying pan that didn't have bacon grease in it. Daniel loved an old-fashioned breakfast. Cooking for him had been part of their routine since they met in college.

Putting the plate of food beside his paper, Colleen waited for a response. When none came, she drew her mouth into a rigid line. She never challenged Daniel, never complained. But when it came to Scotty, Colleen sometimes gathered her courage to speak.

"Did you hear me?"

Daniel looked up. "What?"

"I said I wished you'd take a break and come to Scotty's birthday party tomorrow."

"You know I can't," Daniel said. "I have a big exam in two weeks."

"I know." Colleen's shoulders slumped. "I was hoping you'd find the time. Scotty only turns three once. You're always studying and away from home."

"We've discussed this, Colleen. My education comes first. It's important to this family."

Colleen surveyed him with disappointment. He had already turned his attention back to the newspaper. Her husband was doing his best. Becoming a doctor like his father was important to Daniel—to all of them. She fought back a stab of guilt. She shouldn't complain. It wasn't good to nag. She needed to be supportive.

"Aren't you going to eat your breakfast?" Colleen asked with a sigh.

"What?" Daniel glanced up again. "Oh, yes. Sure."

He laid down the paper and slowly moved the breakfast plate in front of him. Colleen noticed his hands shake as he picked up a slice of bacon.

"I don't think you're getting enough sleep." The observation simply slipped out because it was natural for her to worry.

"I'm okay," he mumbled, stabbing at his eggs like Scotty played with his oatmeal. "I have to study, you know?"

"Yes, I know."

Still Colleen felt a niggling disquiet. She didn't like the way her husband looked. She hated to see him pushing himself so hard, sacrificing so much for them.

Letting out a big breath that was too much like another sigh, Colleen turned back to the kitchen sink and dunked the skillet into the hot, soapy water. She would double down on her efforts. She'd try harder to make life go easier for Daniel—his home life, which was the only thing she could control.

And she silently vowed again not to hassle her husband.

After finishing with cleanup, Colleen lifted Scotty from his booster seat. "Let's go get ready, pumpkin. Grandpa and Nana are waiting for us."

Before she left the kitchen, Colleen looked once more at the man she'd married with such joy only four years earlier. Daniel stared at his plate of food. He'd hardly eaten a thing.

~

Saturday Afternoon
Heritage Springs, Kentucky

SCOTTY SCOOTED OFF his mother's lap and ran after the soccer ball Rob kicked across the grass. Kelly Scott's grandson had changed from a toddler into a little boy almost over night.

She smiled as she lifted a frosty glass of lemonade and sipped the cold liquid from a straw. She loved her two guys so much. Her husband Rob was turning into a wonderful grandfather. He would have been a wonderful father too. She set the glass down on the picnic table, refusing to let out a sigh of remorse.

The past was the past. She'd learned to let it lie. Or at least she tried not to allow guilt consume her. Kelly refused to think about "if only." Sure, she'd had choices. But at eighteen, she'd thought her options limited. If only she'd had more courage, more self-esteem, she would have spoken up—should have spoken up. If she had, maybe she wouldn't have raised her daughter Colleen as a single mom. Maybe Colleen would have known her father before she was a woman grown and married.

Kelly slid her gaze over to her daughter. They sat together on the stone patio under the shade of a canvas awning, the canopy keeping the worst of the July sun from their faces. Scotty's birthday gifts had been opened and the chocolate cake and ice cream eaten. It was good to relax a minute. Good to sit.

Her daughter was so beautiful. C.B.—Colleen as she liked to be called now—was tall like her father with Rob's blond good looks. She had a pert little nose and two cute dimples that appeared when she smiled. Pregnancy and childbirth had made a genuine woman out of her, rounding her figure from the slender shape of her teen years. It was nice Daniel had found a way to keep Colleen at home. His mother had been a stay-at-home

4

mom, raising four children. Daniel had made it clear he expected to do the same for Colleen and his family.

"I'm sorry Daniel couldn't make it today," Kelly said.

Colleen glanced at her mother and then quickly looked away. "He's studying."

"Yes, I know. Still, Scotty only has one three-year-old birthday party."

"Mom, don't start."

Kelly didn't want to start, but a mother's sixth sense told her something was wrong. Daniel's schoolwork had reached a crisis point six months earlier with medical school becoming a huge ordeal. At that time, he'd asked Colleen if she and Scotty could leave the house on weekends so he could study in quiet. Trying to save money and do as Daniel asked, Colleen had driven to Heritage Springs every weekend since then and stayed with Rob and Kelly in their upstairs loft.

Kelly was glad to see Scotty and her daughter so often, but her hospitality was wearing a little thin. Darn it! Sometimes she wanted the weekends to herself. She and Rob were almost newly-weds too. And with her husband busy during the week with his law practice, Kelly selfishly thought she didn't spend enough time with him.

But she had deprived Rob of watching Colleen grow up. For the life of her, she wasn't about to say "no" to her daughter's request. Besides, Rob got such a kick out of pretending to be Scotty's father on weekends.

Rob was with their little grandson so much he was taking the place of the child's father.

The thought jarred Kelly. Her mouth suddenly felt dry. She reached for the glass of lemonade. The bitter liquid went down her throat, cooling it, but not her annoyance. In the yard, Rob kicked the ball, and Scotty chased it, trying to mimic his grandfather and boot it back.

"It's almost five o'clock," Kelly said in what she hoped was a conversational tone as she turned her gaze back to Colleen. "If you left soon, you might surprise Daniel at home, and he'd have an hour or two with Scotty before bedtime."

Her daughter looked irritated. Kelly was interfering. But it was her prerogative, wasn't it? It came with being a mother and wanting her daughter to grow a backbone. For whatever reason, Colleen always deferred to Daniel. Kelly had tried to accept the submissiveness that had come with Colleen's relationship with Daniel. But she didn't like it one bit.

Colleen lifted her chin. "Daniel is studying."

"All day?"

"Yes. He needs the quiet time to prepare for a big exam."

Kelly returned her gaze to the backyard playing field. Rob scooped Scotty up in his arms and gave him a big hug and kiss.

"I'm glad Rob gets time to enjoy Scotty," Kelly said with a soft sigh. She swirled the lemonade in her glass. "He didn't have time with you to watch you grow up. I'm sorry Daniel is missing all this quality time with his son."

"He'll have plenty of time when he finishes med school," Colleen was quick to respond.

"Well, I hope so," Kelly said. "For Scotty's sake."

Kelly glanced at her daughter. Colleen's mouth was drawn into a thin line. Kelly recognized that look of displeasure. Whether it was with Daniel or with her suggestion, Kelly couldn't guess.

She looked toward the yard where Rob had put Scotty on his shoulders and trotted around, the child giggling and squealing with glee. No need to press Colleen. The scene in front of them told the story Kelly had tried to convey. Scotty was growing up without his real father.

THE SETTING SUN made a splash of orange on the horizon and a sharp glare on her windshield. Colleen felt breathless with excitement and a nagging fear. She was going home. Would her early return please Daniel?

As much as she hated to admit it, her mother was right. Daniel should be with his son on his birthday, even for a small amount of time.

Yet, by deciding to go home, she'd surprised even herself.

Thirty minutes after her mother's comment, Colleen had made up her mind after watching Rob play ball with Scotty. Oh, she knew what her mother was doing. Kelly didn't often interfere, and she meant well this time. If Colleen hadn't been convinced in the rightness of her mother's suggestion, she would never have chosen to go against Daniel's wishes.

Would he be angry? The old Daniel wouldn't. But she didn't know this new husband of hers. Sometimes she wished he'd quit med school, but that wouldn't happen. Often she wondered if she had what it took to be the wife of a doctor. Was she too needy? Her mother-in-law, also a doctor's wife, was a lonely, depressed woman. Colleen didn't want to be like that.

It was hard to admit something was wrong with her marriage. As sad as that thought seemed, Colleen realized it was true. These days, her relationship with Daniel was on the backburner. Four years ago, if she'd known how distant Daniel would become, she'd have said "no way."

But in reality, she had changed too. She was a mother first. Now she understood Kelly's fierce protectiveness. When she was a child, Colleen had never known her father. It had hurt terribly. But her mother had been there. Always. Colleen had wondered if it was because of guilt. Maybe her mother was making up for the lack of a dad in her life.

Lately, she'd come to understand her mother's reaction was a maternal thing—the mama bear protecting her cub. That's the way she felt about Scotty. She'd do anything for him.

Colleen had been an adult when she'd met her father. After learning the reason her mother and Rob never married, she understood, but with an adult's reasoning. The child in her never got over the lack of a father. Having Rob in her life today didn't make up for the lost years. The same thing wouldn't happen to her son, she vowed.

Glancing to the backseat, Colleen smiled to herself. Scotty had fallen asleep quickly with his little head slumped over against the high back of the booster seat. The day had been jam-packed with activities leaving the boy exhausted. Regrettably, Daniel wouldn't have much time to see him, because she'd need to put Scotty to bed soon after they arrived home.

Colleen stopped at a four-way stop sign, waited a beat to check for oncoming traffic, and then turned left into her subdivision. It was an old development with modest brick homes and mature trees. A few boats were parked in driveways and an occasional RV. The subdivision was perfect for couples starting out with plenty of neighborhood kids and home prices low enough to be affordable for first time homebuyers. Having no house payment had made it possible for her to be a stay-at-home mom. She had used her inheritance from her great-aunt to pay off their home loan.

Traveling at the mandatory twenty-five mile per hour speed limit, Colleen drove her SUV around the first turn of an S-curve. She couldn't see well. The growing twilight, coupled by shade trees and the sun now hitting her back window, challenged her vision. She shoved her sunglasses onto her head and squinted as a motorcycle rounded the top of the S-curve and sped toward her.

What the heck? She was in her own driving lane, wasn't she? The motorcycle, with two people riding, veered into her path and drove straight toward her Honda.

"Oh, my God!" Colleen stamped on her brakes as the motorcycle smashed into the side panel of her vehicle. Her car screeched to a halt.

Heart in her throat, her hands shaking, Colleen hastily looked back at her son. Asleep. Not hurt.

"Oh, my God," she said once more in a breathless moan. Then she opened the driver's side door.

The driver with the motorcycle on top of him was on the ground near the back wheel of her SUV. A blond woman, wearing a striped black and white outfit—like a prisoner's suit from an old-fashioned movie—was on her feet bending over the wrecked vehicle.

"Oh, my God." Colleen put one foot on the pavement and held on the edge of the open door for dear life. "Are you okay? Are you hurt?"

"I'm not hurt," the costume-clad woman responded in a gravelly voice. "But I think the cycle is busted."

"What about him?" Colleen swung her other foot out of the car but continued sitting. She was too shaken to stand.

The woman winced. She tugged at the handlebar, lifting the bike off the guy, who lay on his side facing the rear of the car. "Baby, are you okay?"

Were they going to a costume party? The man was dressed in a white jumpsuit like Elvis Presley used to wear. Colleen couldn't see him well in the fading light. He pushed against the pavement with one hand and levered himself to his feet. With his back to the car, he staggered across the road to the grass where he collapsed.

"He's hurt!" Colleen said with a gasp. She reached for her smartphone. "I'm calling 911."

"No, honey! Don't do that!" The woman approached her, gesturing with her hands. "Just pull up a little so I can get the bike out from under your back tire."

"But I should call the police. An ambulance."

"No, honey. Don't do that. We're okay."

Colleen fought to keep her teeth from chattering. Nothing like this had ever happened to her. Had she swerved into the path of the motorcycle and struck these two people? It was unreal. Like a sick dream.

But she did as she was asked. Turning back to the steering wheel, she shifted into drive, moving forward a foot or two. She felt the crunch of the bike under her tire. What would Daniel say? Thankfully they had insurance, but if she'd hurt these people, no telling what kind of trouble she'd be in.

Colleen put the Honda into park and turned off the engine. Scotty remained sound asleep. She swallowed hard. Opening her car door, she forced herself to step out. She grabbed her phone. The female "prisoner" tugged at the motorcycle. Its wheel was busted, and gas leaked onto the pavement.

"I need to get this off the road," the woman said, holding the bike up by one handlebar. "Help me, will you?"

"Okay." What more could she do? She'd caused this wreck. And what if the guy in the jumpsuit was hurt?

Colleen grabbed a handlebar and with the woman hauled the motorcycle forward. It wouldn't roll. At the other side of the road they let go, letting the damaged bike drop to the grass.

"You don't need to call the cops," the woman told her again. "We're okay."

How could the woman know? The man could be suffering internal injuries. "I think I need to call the police," she said. Her father was a lawyer. He'd help sort this out.

"No. Don't do that." The man spoke for the first time. He sat in the grass with his head in his hands. "You don't want to do that."

Something wasn't right. Colleen's breath hitched. She took a step nearer to the man. "Are you okay?"

When he lifted his head, he stared back at her with bloodshot eyes.

"Oh, my God!" Colleen inhaled. "Daniel?"

CHAPTER TWO

It *was* Daniel. Dressed in a fancy, but stained jumpsuit with a companion dressed as a convict, he stared back at her with glassy eyes. His hair was disheveled. He reeked of alcohol.

"Daniel?" She could hardly say his name. The words came out in almost a whisper. "What are you doing here?"

"Oh, God, baby, is this your old lady?"

Daniel's gaze shifted from Colleen to the woman. He nodded.

Shock hardened in Colleen's chest. She fought the urge to be sick. What was happening? This couldn't be her beloved husband. Not with this horrible, bleached-blond woman wearing some sort of macabre costume. And what was Daniel doing dressed like Elvis Presley? He was supposed to be home studying.

Colleen's head spun. She couldn't make sense of what was happening, because what was happening didn't make sense.

"Are you hurt?" Colleen asked. Somehow reasonableness won out in her mind. First things first. If Daniel was hurt, he needed medical attention. She held up her cell phone. "Let me call 911."

"No!" They both cried in unison.

"Really, Colleen, I'm okay," Daniel said. He turned to the woman. "Get me up, babe."

The woman clutched Daniel's arm and helped him climb to his feet. He staggered and took a step toward Colleen. For the first time in her life, she backed away from him.

"Take me home, Colleen. I'll be okay."

Fear flooded her. He acted so strange. She didn't want this drunken man riding in the car with her son.

"I don't understand, Daniel," she murmured. "Why are you like this? What are you doing with this woman?"

Seeming to forget her, Daniel turned back to the motorbike and wobbled toward it.

"It's busted, baby" the woman said again. "Damn it. How are we going to get around?"

The woman put an arm around Daniel's shoulder to steady him. In that moment, Colleen's stomach nosedived. She opened her mouth to object to the woman embracing her husband, but nothing came out. What was she going to do? What could she do?

And then suddenly, the situation was out of her control. A police siren wailed in the distance.

The woman whirled around and shot an accusing glare at Colleen. "She called the cops!"

"No, I didn't!"

The two women battled each other silently for another beat.

Then a man ran out of a nearby house dressed in pajamas and bathrobe. "I saw what happened," he shouted. "I've called for help."

The neighbor hurried to Daniel, who had fallen to the ground once more. As the neighbor leaned over her husband, Colleen took another step backwards. Then another. She retreated to her car and glanced in the backseat to find Scotty thankfully asleep. A police car pulled up behind her Honda, and a woman officer climbed out, heading toward the wrecked bike and Daniel.

A second car arrived. "Are you hurt" a male officer asked Colleen as he opened his door.

She shook her head no and then motioned toward Daniel. "He

might be." The policeman turned toward the other officer interviewing the two motorcycle riders. He probably didn't hear Colleen mutter, "He's my husband."

In a fog of disbelief, Colleen watched the surreal scene of Daniel talking to the police. This couldn't be happening. Her carefully crafted world couldn't be crumbling in such a weird way.

But it was.

And she knew it deep in her heart.

KELLY FROWNED as the pictures on the TV flashed silently in front of her. She sat in the living room of Colleen's cute bungalow with the sound on mute. It was too quiet. A brooding oppression settled around her like an unwelcome guest. She pulled her great-aunt's handmade afghan over her lap, tucking her bare toes under its warmth.

The summer night was hot, but Kelly was cold—as cold as the vacant stare in her daughter's eyes.

"Do you want me to check on Scotty?" she asked to break the silence.

Colleen's gaze flicked her way, and she shook her head, not replying. They both knew Kelly had checked on Scotty less than thirty minutes earlier.

How could their lives have spiraled so out of control in such a short span of time? What if she'd never insisted on Colleen going home? Life would have remained blissfully the same. Was it better to learn about Daniel like this? Or was ignorance a kinder friend?

As if reading her mind, Colleen finally focused on her mother. "I want a divorce," she said in a dead voice.

"Don't be too hasty." Kelly didn't want Colleen to do something she'd regret later.

"You didn't see him, Mom." Colleen sucked in a tear-filled breath, but her eyes were uncharacteristically dry given the circumstances. "You didn't see him with that slut. He called her 'babe' right in front of me."

What could she say? Kelly didn't want to defend her son-in-law, not after the stunt he'd pulled that night. But she feared it was more than a stunt. Hell, after Colleen's graphic description, it seemed as if it was more like Daniel's regular pattern of behavior.

"How could he do it, Mom?" Colleen's voice broke Kelly's heart. "How could he lie to me? Endanger our son? Be with that woman?"

"I don't know, honey. You said he was drunk."

"Or on drugs." Colleen covered her face with her hands and spoke into them. "I don't know him. I don't know what he's become."

A car pulled into the driveway. Kelly stood and padded quietly to the window. "It's your father."

She opened the door for Rob and fell into his arms. He hugged her tightly and kissed the top of her head.

"What happened?" Kelly wanted to know, stepping aside to let the man she loved enter the room.

Rob walked straight to Colleen, who sat huddled in a worn easy chair. He knelt and took her hands into his. Her daughter's eyes clouded, and the first tear slid down her cheek. "What happened?"

"I saw him in jail. I said I was his lawyer, and they gave me access."

"How was he?" Kelly asked.

"Sobering up." Rob glanced up. "Slowly. He has to stay the night, but I think I can get him out tomorrow morning. He's in big trouble."

"I won't press charges," Colleen whispered. "He's my husband, no matter what."

"Then it may go easier on him, but driving drunk is still a punishable offense."

"But it was his first time, wasn't it?" Kelly asked.

Rob grimaced, not answering, and she knew she was wrong. How many drunk driving charges did their son-in-law have, for goodness sakes?

"Dr. Lyons came in as I was leaving. He told me he'd get Daniel all the help he needs. He's aware his son has a drinking problem." Rob climbed to his feet. "It appears that Mrs. Lyons is a recovering alcoholic herself. So the family has had experience with such matters."

"Now the skeletons come out of the closet." Kelly's voice was hard, more critical than she wanted it to be.

"It gets even worse," Rob said, his voice hushed. "Dr. Lyons made phone calls to his contacts at the university. It looks as if Daniel flunked out his last semester. He hasn't been enrolled in school for over six months."

The truth was difficult to hear. Kelly drew in a long breath. "So all this extra studying and weekend time alone was simply a cover-up."

Rob nodded, as if unable to say more.

Under her breath, Colleen muttered, "He lied to me."

Glancing at Colleen, Kelly longed to wrap arms around her daughter and comfort her as she had done when she was a little girl. But her daughter was an adult. A mother herself. And tonight she'd grown remote, unapproachable.

"We'll stay with you tonight," Rob said. "I'll go with you to pick Daniel up in the morning."

Colleen sat silently then lifted her chin. She wiped the lone tear from her face. "You can help me the most if you take Scotty home with you in the morning. Take his clothes. His toys." She swallowed, the line of her jaw firming. "I don't want him here when Daniel comes home. I never want that man around Scotty ever again. He doesn't deserve to be a father. He doesn't deserve to have a son like Scotty."

Kelly thought Colleen would break down, but she didn't. Kelly did. A sob escaped her lips, and she turned her back, hiding the tears that filled her eyes. God, what an awful thing to have happened to her beloved daughter? How terrible for Scotty, for that precious little boy.

"We'll do that, Colleen," Rob said in a calm, measured voice. "If that is what you want us to do."

"It is."

Colleen's words held finality. Kelly glanced back at her husband and their daughter. She clenched her jaw in anguish.

"Will you do me another favor, Daddy?"

"Anything, sweetheart."

"I want you to file the paperwork. I want a divorce."

CHAPTER THREE

Nine Months Later
Heritage Springs, Kentucky

"What am I going to do, Rob?" James Madison asked. He toured Rob Scott's law office in four steps, turned, and stalked the other way.

His friend and attorney sat behind a mahogany desk and in front of a floor-to-ceiling bookshelf filled with leather-bound legal tomes. The look on Rob's face was sympathetic, but annoyed, as if he couldn't understand the full extent of Jamie's angst.

Perhaps Jamie couldn't understand it himself. Or explain the tightness in his gut at the thought of appearing in public as his alter ego Madison Mallory.

"I'm afraid you'll have to fulfill the obligations of your contract," Rob answered, his voice tight as if controlling his impatience.

"You sound just like a lawyer."

"That's what you pay me for."

Jamie glared at his attorney. "I thought you were my friend."

Rob rocked back in his chair, stretching out his legs and clasping his hands behind his head. "I am your friend. I simply don't want to see you sued for everything you don't have because you won't fulfill your contract."

"But I can't! My readers think I'm a woman. I can't go on a book tour. They'll know I'm a fraud."

Jamie picked up his pacing. Crap. He'd gotten himself into a real mess. Served him right for not reading his contract closely before he'd signed it. He'd relied on his mother's agent for that. The woman was so glad she was not losing a client that she didn't protect Jamie's true interest.

"I suppose I don't understand the book business." Rob shook his head. "Seems to me if a reader likes your writing, it doesn't matter if you're male or female."

Stopping once more, Jamie drew a frustrated breath. "This is a romance novel. These are romance readers. Women read romance, and they expect women to write the books."

"It doesn't make sense to me," Rob said, sitting forward once more.

Jamie collapsed in a chair facing the desk. The fear in the pit of his stomach was an irrational thing. But he couldn't help it. No one but Rob and this turncoat agent knew he was James Madison, a man—not Madison Mallory, the bestselling female romance author. The publisher didn't know. And, of course, his public didn't know. His website featured scenes of medieval castles and knights in armor. His biography was intentionally vague. The photo of his mother had been taken off the website and did not appear on the back covers of the Madison Mallory books.

He had been an untenured professor of history when his mother was diagnosed with early onset dementia. Divorced, a schoolteacher herself, his mother had no savings to speak of, only her grandmother's house in Heritage Springs. She'd understood right away her only son would struggle to pay for her nursing care. Soon after the diagnosis, she had begged him to keep her dream alive and handed him a dusty box with several complete manuscripts inside.

"These may need some polishing," she'd told him. "I wrote them years ago. They will help you fulfill my new four-book contract."

He'd never imagined his little white lie, told when agreeing to take on his mother's pseudonym, would come back to haunt him.

"I can't reveal my true identity," Jamie said. He heard the hopelessness in his voice.

"Surely, your publisher will understand. They have marketing departments to handle things like smoothing over your true identity."

"There's more to it."

"I'm listening."

"I can let nothing interfere with my royalty income, meager as it is at the moment, because I use it to pay for Mother's care. Nursing homes are expensive."

Rob nodded. "Okay. I understand that. Still, I don't see the problem."

"I need someone to pose as Madison Mallory. I need a surrogate." Jamie stood and paced again, pausing to stare out the long window facing the town square. A blond woman crossed the sidewalk from the courthouse. She walked slowly, distracted by a cell phone in her hand.

"Hire someone. That seems easy enough," Rob offered.

Jamie turned to face his attorney. "But who can I trust? And where do I find someone willing to pretend to be a famous romance writer?"

Rob shrugged. "That I can't help you with."

"I know." Jamie's sigh of frustration filled the room. "And there's more. I'm in a deadline crunch, but this time I've run out of Mother's manuscripts to guide me. I have no clue what I'm doing. No clue at all."

"That I don't believe. You're a bright guy, Jamie. You haven't turned in your mother's manuscripts without rewriting them, making them better. Don't sell yourself short."

Jamie plopped down once more in the chair. "I *can* sell myself short with my typing abilities. It's one reason I never finished my dissertation. I write everything longhand. I need someone to type my manuscripts for me and to transcribe Mother's old books she sold in the nineties. I've gotten her rights back, and I want to self-publish them."

"How did you manage for the last two years then?"

"June Hobson."

"June?" The level of Rob's voice rose in question. "Your next-door neighbor?"

"Yes. She thought they were mother's manuscripts and was glad to type them. I paid her, of course."

"So, what's the problem?"

Jamie scrubbed a hand over his face. "She's moved to Louisville to live with her sister. She thinks she's too old to live alone any longer."

"I see."

But did Rob really see? Did he understand the concern that curled around his gut? He loved his mother. She'd raised him, cared for him, been a mother *and* father to him all his life. There was no way he'd let her down now, even if his life had been turned upside down by his little white lie. Trouble was—he was so deeply into the charade, he needed money so badly—that he saw no way out. He had to continue pretending.

"At least, can you find someone to type for me? I'm desperate."

"Let me see what I can do for you. I'll ask around." Rob stood up. The appointment time was over. "As for your other problem, I'm afraid I don't know how to help you with that one."

Jamie climbed to his feet. "That's fine. Thank you."

They shook hands, and Jamie left the office, shutting the door behind him. He smiled at the secretary and headed outside. As he stepped through the outer door, a woman with her head buried in her cell phone crashed into him.

"Oof!" He caught her upper arms, steadying her. "Watch where you're going, honey."

She shook herself free, turning angry blue eyes up at him. "Don't you *honey* me, buster."

It was the woman he'd seen crossing the street. "Sorry, but you ran into me. You should pay more attention to what's going on around you, not your stupid cell phone."

"It's none of your business what I do with my cell phone."

"It is when you run into me because you're so obtuse about how your actions impact other people."

"Well!" she said fuming.

He bowed slightly and touched his brow, pretending to tip a hat. "My pardon," he said, "but I have more important things to do than to argue with you."

With that, he slipped around the rude woman and left the office. Taking a deep breath of the spring air, he heard his mother's voice inside his head telling him he had been just as rude as the young woman and another voice saying the blonde sure was cute.

"WELL! OF ALL THE NERVE." The blond woman entered the office and turned her ire on the secretary. "Men! I swear, Gail, I can do without *all* of them."

Gail ducked her head, hiding a smile. "Except for your dad, I suppose."

C.B. let out a huff of air, coming down from her high horse. "Yes, my dad is a jewel. Let's just hope I can raise my son to be just like him."

Gail nodded in agreement. "I hear you're doing a wonderful job. Your dad sure is proud of Scotty."

"That he is." C.B. inclined her head toward the door. "Is he busy?"

"No, that was his last appointment before lunch."

C.B. took the secretary's comment as the go-ahead to walk into her father's office. She tapped lightly on the door and let herself in.

"Colleen, baby!" Rob sprang from his seat and came around his desk, giving her a hug. "To what do I owe this pleasure? I'm so glad to see you."

"As if you don't see enough of me and Scotty," C.B. said and returned her dad's hug.

"Have a seat." He waved his hand toward the chair facing his desk and walked around it to sit down. "Oh, I forgot. You want to be called C.B. now. My bad."

"That's fine. It's just that C.B. seems to fit me better at this stage of my life."

Her mother had always called her C.B. for Colleen Baron, that is until she'd married Daniel and insisted on becoming Colleen. In her way of thinking then, she'd changed her life by marrying into the Lyons family. In her mind, it had been time for a new identity. Daniel had agreed. Now divorced from the scumbag, she had opted to keep his last name for Scotty's sake, but she didn't have to remain "Colleen."

"Aren't you and Scotty coming over for dinner tonight?" Rob asked as he straightened papers on his desk.

"Yes, but I wanted to talk to you alone."

Rob paused, shoved the papers aside, and looked up. "I'm all ears."

C.B. grinned at that. Her dad was so open and inviting. So easy to get along with. The love for her was written all over his face, and she was thankful for it. He'd been her rock these last nine months since the Daniel Disaster.

"I'm going crazy, Daddy." She saw concern in his eyes after she made her confession.

"But I thought you liked living above the carriage house with Scotty."

"It's not that." C.B. took a deep breath. How did she put her discontent into words? Her parents had been so good to Scotty and her, letting them live in their cabin with them for a couple of months and then converting the carriage house at the B&B into two apartments, one for Bekah Morgan and her girls and one for her. "I'm bored."

"Bored?"

"Yes, Bekah doesn't need me to help run the bed and breakfast. She's quite capable on her own. There are never more than three couples at a time anyway."

Rob was so easy to read. He was afraid she wanted to leave town. He had missed out on her growing up and was afraid he'd miss out on Scotty's childhood too. That was the last thing she planned, however. She simply needed more to do.

"I went to college and have a degree in communications. Before marrying Daniel, I had a nice entry-level job in a marketing department." C.B. shrugged. "I'd just like to go back to doing something I'm passionate about. Helping Bekah at the B&B doesn't cut it. Besides, her girls are old enough to help her too."

Rob rubbed his chin. "I see."

"But there's nothing in Heritage Springs. And I don't want to move. I just want something to do."

"Really?" Rob sat back in his chair. "I may have just the right thing for you."

"You do?" C.B. brightened. "I'd love to find a job nearby, one where I could work with a woman. Gran used to work with Sally at the antiques store downtown. But I don't think I'm into retail."

Rob's eyebrows puckered. "I was going to say I have the perfect job for you."

C.B. perked up. "What is it?"

Her father stood and went to the window staring out with

unseeing eyes. Then, as if he'd made up his mind, he turned around to face her. "Have you ever heard of Madison Mallory?"

"The bestselling writer?"

"Yes. She happens to live across the street from the B&B. In the house next to June Hobson's."

"You've got to be kidding. We never see anyone come or go from that house. Bekah says the person who lives there goes in and out through the back alley entrance."

Rob hesitated. "The house belonged to Eva Mallory, Madison Mallory's mother, I believe."

"Oh, I see the connection."

"Madison Mallory is a client of mine. Very reclusive. He—'er —she is on deadline and needs help typing manuscripts and transcribing copies of old books."

C.B. leaned forward. "Interesting."

"It would give you something to do in the short term." Rob spoke more quickly. "And it's right across the street from the B&B. You could work at your own pace, I'm sure. And with Scotty in preschool two days a week and your mother willing to babysit, you'd have time."

This job, more part-time than what she'd hoped for, was a start. She'd taken her time to heal from Daniel's debacle, and now she wanted to move on. Maybe a job with a famous romance author was just the ticket to her way out of the doldrums of divorce.

"I'll do it. When do I start?"

Rob gave her that charming smile that had won her mother's heart. "Perfect! Probably tomorrow, but I'll check and let you know."

Her father rose and hastily ushered her out of his office as if he didn't want her to change her mind. That wouldn't happen. Once she'd made it up, she didn't change it.

CHAPTER FOUR

"It's you!"

Jamie opened his door to find the obnoxious woman from yesterday standing on his front porch. She wore a dark blue skirt and a white blouse, so thin he could see the outline of her bra underneath. Her blond hair was tied back from her face, giving it a severe look, not like the impertinent beauty from yesterday who'd had pretty wavy hair.

She pulled herself up and straightened her shoulders. "I have an appointment with Madison Mallory. I'm supposed to work for her."

"And I'm expecting Rob Scott's daughter."

"That's me," she said with a proud inflection. "C.B. Lyons. Is Miss Mallory at home?"

Rob was discrete, but was he so discrete that he hadn't told his daughter that *he* was Madison Mallory?

"Come in." Jamie stepped aside to let Rob's daughter pass into the foyer. She was a good ten years younger than he and sexy to a fault. When she brushed past, he caught the alluring scent of lavender, his favorite.

Turning to face him in the entrance hall, she looked up. Her eyes were apprehensive. They were also bright blue and quite enticing. He couldn't meet her gaze and dropped his to stare at his bare feet. He must appear a mess—white T-shirt, blue jean cut-offs, a day's growth of beard. Sometimes when he was writing, he lost himself. It happened when he wasn't writing too.

He shifted his stance and glanced up. "What did Rob tell you?"

She set her jaw. "He told me Madison Mallory needed someone to type for her. I have a college degree in communications. That's one thing I can do—type."

"You're perfect then." But why did he sense she wasn't perfect? Her confrontational attitude was off-putting. Her persona was much too sensual. For the first time in a lifetime, he found the inkling of attraction stir in his stone-cold heart.

Back in the day, his former fiancée Julia had accused him of not having a heart, of being incapable of expressing emotion. She wanted more from a relationship, she'd told him the night she handed back his engagement ring and walked away. How many years ago had that been? Fifteen? From that moment, he'd shut down his under-developed heart, concealed his feelings of failure and rejection, suppressed his loneliness, and concentrated on his college classes and doctoral dissertation, until he wrote romance novels to support his mother. How ironic was that?

"I must apologize for yesterday," he said. "I had a lot on my mind, finding a typist being one of them, but that's no excuse."

"You were rather discourteous," she acknowledged, seeming uncertain about her position.

"And you weren't watching where you were going."

"I was checking on my son. My mother wanted to know about his next doctor's appointment."

"Can't you call on the phone?"

"I could, if I wanted to."

It wasn't his place to question her lifestyle. He kicked himself mentally for the lapse. "I suppose not being able to type, I don't care for texting," he admitted grudgingly.

She inclined her head as if a light bulb had just gone off somewhere. "Wait a minute. Are you Madison Mallory?"

"Yes. It's my pseudonym. My real name is James Madison."

"James Madison?"

"Like the president, founding father, and writer of the Federalist Papers." He grinned at her confused expression. "But most people call me Jamie."

"I don't understand. I thought Madison Mallory was a woman."

"She was." How much did he reveal about his mother's illness? He was private and preferred to keep his mother safe and secure, away from the prying eyes of the press. Who knew what would happen if the tabloids found out about her? "But it is also a penname. I'm Madison Mallory now."

She glared at him as if letting the information sink in. Then letting out a huff, she swept past him toward the door. "Well, I can't work for you!"

He grabbed her arm. "Hold up! Why not?"

She stopped and frowned at his hand. It was the second time in as many days that he'd touched her. Another *faux pas*. He loosened his grasp and stepped back.

"Because you're a man," she snapped. "Because of that." She indicated his hand with an irritated shake of her head.

"I guarantee, Miss Lyons, I'm a true gentleman. You have nothing to fear from me."

That she even implied he might not be a gentleman was unsettling. Even Julia had found him courteous, respectful. In fact, she'd accused him of being too genteel, lacking real passion. He supposed she was right. He was naturally reserved, an introvert not an extrovert. Although loving Julia, he'd not been able to give her what she needed. Expressing emotion had been hard.

Maybe that was what was wrong with this damn manuscript he was trying to write. Maybe without his mother's plots and inspiration, he didn't have what it took to carry on her dream.

"I have yet to see proof of that, Mr. Madison."

He let out a slow breath. "We have gotten off on the wrong foot."

"To say the least."

"If you give me another chance," he said, running his hand through his mop of prematurely gray hair, "I promise to do better. I really need you, Miss Lyons."

She stared at him, chewing on her lower lip. Was she making up her mind about him? He grinned sheepishly. Couldn't she see he was a good guy?

"I'll give you a chance," she said. "I want the work."

"Wonderful! When can you start?"

"Now, if you need me to. I came prepared to stay."

Jamie's pulse raced. Why was that? This woman was going to be his employee, nothing more. But some sixth sense thrummed hard in his chest, warning him to be careful, challenging him not to make another heartbreaking mistake like he'd made with the regretted and long-departed Julia.

C.B. STARED at the rather disheveled man who looked out of place in the formal, nineteenth-century foyer. Eva Mallory's home was larger than the original one her grandparents had owned across the street, the one her parents had converted into a bed and breakfast after her grandmother remarried and moved. Even with twelve-foot ceilings, this entryway was gloomy. It had dark wood floors and heavy ornate furniture. An antique, mahogany, bow-front chest of drawers stood in the hall and a staircase curved overhead to the second floor, blocking the light. Only the tall and narrow glass sidelights next to the door provided illumination, but they were covered with sheer white curtains, allowing only weak light to enter.

Through the dimness, she glared back at the writer. She didn't like the way this man looked at her. There was a duality in his expression, as if maybe he was sizing her up professionally as well as checking her out sexually. Did she trust him? Was he really who he said he was? But he was a client of her father's. He couldn't be that bad, could he?

Come to think of it, she now had a bone to pick with her father. He knew she'd had it with men. Why had Rob sent her to this job?

Duh. Because she'd asked for something to do.

It made sense, but not the fact that her father failed to tell her the truth. Madison Mallory had turned out to be a man—a very handsome, though unkempt man. He hadn't been this scruffy yesterday when he'd left her father's office and been rude to her. Did she really want a job with such a hunk for a boss?

"Let me show you where you'll work," he said, turning on his heel and heading down the hallway to the back of the house.

C.B. let out a big sigh. What choice did she have? Boredom was not something she liked, especially with Scotty in preschool and her days growing long. Even this typing gig would be better than twiddling her thumbs.

Hurrying to catch her new employer, she glimpsed a very stiff living room opening off the foyer. It was replete with polished antique furniture and stuffed sofas and papered with green vines and flying yellow birds. The room probably looked the same as when its former owner had lived there. Hopefully, the rest of the house was not as sad and depressing as the front rooms.

It wasn't. Off to one side of the back hallway was a thoroughly remodeled, open-concept kitchen with stainless steel appliances. The hall opened up into a bright, inviting sunroom, but her new employer turned left into an equally charming office, in what looked to have, on one occasion, been the dining room.

He stopped suddenly and turned to face her. Once more she slammed into him.

Catching her by the arms, he hesitated, gazing down at her,

giving her another going-over. She felt a tingle—in her arms, where he touched her and in her heart, which skipped a beat. There was a pregnant pause while some sort of strange connection vibrated between them.

Then C.B. shook herself free and moved back. She didn't offer an excuse, and he didn't explain his piercing appraisal and the warm safety of his hands.

"This is my office," he finally said and turned away from her, going to his desk.

Aqua walls enlivened the office, and a two-tone cream and taupe area rug added a textured, mazelike pattern on top of the wooden floor. A leather, custom sofa nestled under a tall window masked by white plantation shutters. Built-in bookshelves lined the two parallel walls at the far end of the room.

His desk was a large mahogany table littered with papers and books. They were scattered on the floor too. His workspace looked as disheveled as its owner. Standing at the desk, he sifted through papers and completely forgot her presence.

"A-hmm." She cleared her throat.

His head snapped up. "Oh, yes, Miss Lyons."

"It's Mrs. Lyons, but you may call me C.B."

His cockeyed grin was charming.

"Ah, yes. And you may call me Jamie." He glanced down at his desk again. "As you can see, C.B., I am in great need of organization here."

"Apparently."

Still looking at his desk, he grinned again at the dryness of her remark. "Hmm. Let me see. While I organize these manuscript papers, you can begin by transcribing the text of this galley proof."

Jamie picked up a manila-mailing envelope from a dusty pile on the floor. When he handed it to her, C.B. read the return address—New York City. Inside was the unbound text of a completed romance novel written by Madison Mallory.

"You don't have this digitally?"

"No. The rights to several books were returned. Any electronic copy has been lost. I found copies of the old galleys in my…'er…in a file cabinet."

Odd, especially in today's age when everything was digital. But C.B. guessed if he didn't like to type, then he'd probably never kept anything online. Heck, he may have used an old fashioned typewriter when he wrote his first book.

"I believe these were typed on an electric typewriter," he admitted when he caught her staring. Did he read minds? "That was high technology in its day."

"I imagine." C.B. couldn't help but be skeptical. If this guy didn't like to type, why in the heck was the original manuscript typed on a typewriter? That was even harder than using a computer and a keyboard.

There was an awkward moment, as if Jamie knew she didn't believe him. Then he drew himself up. "Nevertheless," he said, taking control again. "This has to be put into a Word document. I intend to republish the novel. I've hired a service to set up the book and help me self-publish it. But first, the manuscript must be in digital format."

"This seems easy enough," C.B. said.

"There are fifteen of them."

She lifted an eyebrow. "Really? I guess you're stuck with me awhile then."

"It seems so."

More eye contact. C.B. chewed her lower lip as she wondered about the prickling of her skin and the fluttering in her belly. This wouldn't do. Not one bit.

"So, do you have a computer?" She didn't see one anywhere.

He caught his breath. "Yes. Let me find it."

Finding it took a minute or two, but he finally pulled a laptop case from under a stack of papers on the sofa. When he handed it to her, C.B. carefully avoided any physical contact. She was no longer the naïve young girl who'd fell in love with Daniel Lyons. She had gained a healthy distrust of most men, especially sexy ones with piercing blue eyes.

"Where can I work?"

He pointed to his messy desk. "How about at the end of the table?"

"Oh, no. How about the sunroom I saw? Maybe you have a table in there."

"Yes, that's fine."

He turned back to the desk in question and rifled through more papers, dismissing her. His overt rejection stung. One moment they'd had some sort of vibe going on and the next he was back to business like an absent-minded professor. *C'est la vie*.

Yet the sunroom was a pleasant surprise. The room was bright and cheery. Painted white with two white French doors leading to a stone outdoor patio, a bank of windows let light stream onto a patterned blue and yellow tile floor. Blue fabric covered a comfy sofa and chairs.

C.B. found a table and chairs near one of the windows and set up shop. How did he want the manuscript formatted? Figuring there was no way Jamie would have a clue, C.B. fixed the margins at one inch all around, turned on double spacing, and created a file for *The Scottish Captive Bride*.

Soon, as her fingers flew across the keyboard, she was lost in the highlands of Scotland with an imprisoned female and her harsh, but hunky captor. Sort of true to life, wasn't it?

CHAPTER FIVE

"It sounds thoroughly romantic to me," Bekah Morgan said as she mixed a batch of blueberry muffins. That day the B&B entertained two couples from Chicago for the start of the Keeneland thoroughbred racing meet and Bekah had promised breakfast to them at eight o'clock. "I've never met a famous author."

"Well, it isn't," C.B. complained. "Romantic, that is. This guy is rude and looks as if he was raised in a barn. Thank goodness he doesn't smell like it."

"I still can't believe he lives across the street. The house seems deserted."

"That's because he spends most of his time in the rear of the house."

C.B. had obsessed over her new working situation all night long. Talking to Bekah eased her anxiety, but she was walking on a thin line by revealing Madison Mallory's identity.

"You mustn't tell anyone," she cautioned. "Before I left yesterday, he made me sign a confidentiality agreement."

"Not a trusting sort, is he?"

"Apparently not."

Bekah ladled the muffin mixture into paper cups inside a

muffin tin. "He seems mysterious. Just knowing he's across the street writing away gives the place a touch of mystery."

"Yes, I suppose I won't be bored now."

"Be careful what you wish for."

Right. But what did she wish for? A new start in life, for sure. That didn't necessarily include a new job with such a frustrating man who raised her ire simply by looking at her with those dreamy eyes.

At that moment, Bekah's two girls Tara and Courtney burst into the kitchen from the outside courtyard and dropped their school backpacks on the floor. C.B. used that moment of chaos to excuse herself. She needed to get Scotty ready for her mom to pick up. She lifted her grumpy three-year-old off the kitchen floor and carried him the short distance to the carriage house and their second floor apartment.

Having family to help out was certainly a blessing. She didn't envy Bekah's lack of kin. The single mom had no support from anyone except C.B.'s mom and dad. That Bekah now ran the B&B had worked out perfectly for both families.

Her mom was on time as usual, so forty-five minutes later, C.B. buckled Scotty into his car seat and gave him a kiss goodbye. Taking a deep breath, C.B. watched Kelly's SUV drive away.

Why did she feel lightheaded as if she'd spun in the Merry Mixer ride at the county fair? She could readily pinpoint the source of her distress—her new job *and* her new employer. It wasn't hard to figure out. Discovering why she was letting him get to her was another matter.

Calm down. Relax. Better get on with the day.

Mustering another deep breath for courage, C.B. headed across Main Street. Was he watching her from his front window? She brushed away goose pimples and the accompanying anxiety.

As soon as she knocked, he opened the door.

"You're on time," he said, avoiding eye contact. He stepped aside to let her enter.

Did he expect her to be late? "You told me eight-thirty."

"I did."

She paused beside him, irritated. In the hazy morning light, he looked better, as if he'd combed his hair. He'd put on shoes too and clean jeans, a long-sleeve gray shirt, and a gray and maroon argyle sweater. Today he gave her the impression of a college professor.

"I intend to earn the money you're going to pay me, Mr. Madison."

"Jamie."

"You told me to be here," she said in a huff, "and I'm on time...Jamie."

"I appreciate that, C.B."

He didn't have any trouble calling her by her nickname. The way he said it sounded charming, intimate, as if he caressed her initials in his head. Daniel had never said her name that way. He'd hated calling her "C.B." and that's why she'd changed it. To please him.

She'd be damned if she'd bend over backwards to please a man again.

But shit! That was exactly what she'd be doing by working for him. The realization almost drove C.B. backwards mentally, but she stood her ground and stared up at the man who annoyed her simply by his presence.

Madison Mallory wasn't technically a man. It was a pseudonym, a nom de plume for a romance writer, not a person who could sweep her off her feet like Daniel had. This man was her employer. She'd do well to remember that.

HAD he imagined that spark thing vibrating between them? Had yesterday's reaction to C.B. been a fluke? Staring at the blond woman who today wore tight jeans and a suggestive, hip-length blouse with a V-neckline and three-quarter sleeves, Jamie felt the same instant awareness that had curled his toes a day earlier. He wanted to reach out and rip that lacey top right off her body and explore what she hid beneath it.

God, he'd written too many romance novels. A sane man didn't think like that.

Jamie turned abruptly and strode to the back of the house. Get a grip, man. A tight, firm grip.

She followed him, of course. He sensed her presence as he had sensed her absence all last night. The house had seemed empty without her in it.

Leading her into the shiny new kitchen, Jamie pointed at the coffeemaker. "We have one of these one-cup things," he said ungraciously.

She didn't seem to mind his ill manners and brushed past him to the counter. "Don't you just love them?" she gushed. "I find them so convenient."

"Yes, it's great." What more could he say when she flipped her long hair away from her face with a sexiness that ripped his best intentions in two. "Make me a cup, will you? I take mine black."

It was more of an order than a request. But he couldn't help himself. He didn't like the feelings she stirred. Retreating to his office, he sank into the chair behind his desk and gave the hand-written pages of his latest manuscript a blank stare.

Jamie jumped when she plopped the coffee mug on the edge of his desk. Liquid spattered on the tabletop.

"Here's your coffee," C.B. said. Was that a snarl in her voice? "Next time, get your own damn coffee. You pay me to type. Not wait on you like a maid."

Touché. He gazed up at her tongue-tied. They studied each other as if doing visual battle. He was definitely the loser in the contest, and he knew it. She had a frown upon her face and the makings of a stress line between her eyebrows. Jamie didn't want to make her unhappy. He didn't want to challenge her, but the way his body strummed when he looked at her, it was safer to go to war than to settle for peace. Or "piece" which was oddly what he wanted at the moment.

He looked away. Good, God. This day was turning into a nightmare.

"Point taken," he grumbled, ignoring her. "Now you'd better get at it."

She left him, still angry he knew by the stomping of her feet. But he had managed to protect himself this one round. If he could only finish his damn manuscript, then he would be done with his attractive hired help. And for the moment that sounded like a very good solution to a problem that had, out-of-the-blue, reared its ugly head.

WHAT A JERK! C.B. pounded out the text of *The Scottish Captive Bride*, racing through the love scene, trying not to follow the sighs and hot and bothered dialogue between the two fictitious lovers.

Who read this stuff anyway? Silly women with no life and time on their hands?

Her fingers paused on the keypad. Women like her?

How sad. How dreadfully sad. Nine months ago she'd been in love, a busy housewife and mother. She'd looked forward to the day when her husband finished his schoolwork and became a doctor. Now she was a pathetic divorcee with no life except that of being a single mother to a precious little boy.

C.B. choked back tears that clogged her throat and threatened to spill down her cheeks. She'd been sorry for herself long enough, dammit. She wouldn't let it get started again.

But really. This book was such a piece of fluff. She could hardly stomach it.

Twenty pages more into the manuscript, when she suspected

she was being watched, C.B. raised her eyes to see her employer standing a few feet away holding another handful of papers. Clouds hid the sun, casting the room into shadows. Her work-space was no longer bright and cheery. In fact, it was about as gloomy as the miserable look on James Madison's face.

"Yes?"

He took a step nearer. "I have my work-in-progress for you to type."

"I'm not finished with the manuscript from yesterday." She couldn't work miracles.

"I need you to start on this one. I have a deadline."

When he didn't move closer, C.B. sat back in the chair and took a deep breath. Honestly, the way he stared at her was off-putting. It gave her the creeps. Or was she lying to herself? Was it more because her heart quickened when he was near? But wasn't that the last thing she wanted. Or was that another lie?

"Do these books really make money?" she asked tipping her head toward the galley pages spread out in front of her.

"You'd be surprised how much," he said, coming over and sitting down across from her. He laid his stack of ruled paper on the table. "Once you get a name and a readership, then it becomes much easier."

"How does that happen?"

"Word of mouth is the best way. Look at some of the popular books that have taken off simply because one reader tells another one. It's the same with movies. If you enjoy a movie, you'll recommend it to your friends."

"That makes sense." Seriously, he had the prettiest blue eyes for a man...if you overlooked the crow's feet that bordered them, making him look distinguished, even intellectual. C.B. berated herself mentally and shoved hair from her forehead. "This book I'm working on was written in the nineties. You must have been a teenager when you wrote it."

"Ah, that's about right." He refused to look her in the eyes.

"Madison Mallory was popular in the heyday of historical romance."

Awkwardness and a long silence followed.

"Well, then." C.B. stood up. "Do you have anything for lunch? If not, I can go home and get something to eat."

He jumped to his feet. "No, don't do that."

It was almost as if he didn't want to let her go. "Well, do you have any peanut butter? Bread? I can make a sandwich."

He grinned then in his charming and most disconcerting way. "I actually made a casserole last night. Chicken and Chinese noodles. Mushroom soup. My mother's recipe. Would you care for leftovers?"

"A man who can cook is a man after my own heart," she quipped.

He hesitated. Her words had startled her. And him. More of that weird connection shifted between them. "I do like to cook," he said after a self-conscious pause.

"It's a wonder a woman let you get away."

Had she said the wrong thing? In an attempt to keep up the banter, she'd said the first thing that entered her mind. By the look on his face, it had been a dumb thing to say.

"Why do you think that?" His voice was low.

"You're not married. So I figure at some point a woman let you slip through her fingers."

He stared at her. "Would that have been a bad thing?"

"I don't know. I'm reserving judgment. I hardly know you."

Jamie turned on his heel and left her. He had a habit of doing that, leaving her standing glaring after him. Well, she was just trying to make conversation. She hadn't planned on hitting a sore spot.

Following him into the kitchen, C.B. watched as Jamie opened the refrigerator door and removed a covered casserole dish. He wouldn't let her help, so she perched on a bar stool and observed his quiet efficiency. What was it with this guy? Had a mysterious lover really dumped him? Did a divorce cause a broken heart? For the first time, she was honestly curious about her employer— the man, not the famous romance writer.

He put a microwaved plate of chicken casserole in front of her and offered her a glass of ice water with lemon to drink. Watching her take the first bite, he seemed to hold his breath.

"How is it?"

She chewed and swallowed. "Actually, it's very good."

Their gazes connected. They smiled at each other. Then he dropped his head and turned around. Was he that shy? He intrigued her.

Before he could join her at the bar, his cell phone chimed, and he dug it from his pocket. "I've got to take this," he said, walking to the window.

She couldn't hear what he said, but his body language changed, as if he was worried. C.B. sipped her water, observing him over the rim of the glass.

Turning back to her a few minutes later, he told her he had to drive to Lexington. Pressing matter. Nothing serious, but it needed attending to.

"When you leave for the day, pull the front door shut," he requested. "It will lock."

"I thought I'd leave around three o'clock."

"Fine."

He was distracted. He didn't even eat his lunch, putting his unwrapped plate into the refrigerator. When he'd gone and she'd finished eating, C.B. washed her plate and covered his with plastic wrap and went back to work. His handwriting was sloppy. It took her a while to figure out the loops and spirals of his cursive writing, but she finally got the hang of it. She started a new computer file for *My Highland Bride* and typed two pages.

Unfortunately, she couldn't stop wondering about the secrecy that seemed to surround her boss. Curiosity, as they say, killed the cat, so she shut the manuscript file and opened the Internet to surf for information about Madison Mallory. Most of what she read was promotional material, and the only picture she found was an old one of a bouffant quaffed, middleaged woman. It made sense for him to fake his photograph, as guarded as he was about identity.

What didn't make sense was her attraction to him. She didn't want to feel it. Not after Daniel. Not after he'd screwed with her brain and assaulted her soul.

CHAPTER SIX

They fell into a pattern. C.B. took Scotty to playschool or her mother picked him up. Then C.B. crossed the street where Jamie always waited for her at the front door. With very few words said between them, they'd go to their respective workspaces where she'd decipher his scrawling cursive handwriting or type the printed text of a galley manuscript into the computer file. Lunch was at noon. She would leave at three o'clock. He'd escort her to the front door, and she'd hear the lock click when he shut the door behind her.

All the while, C.B. soaked up the romance of his novels—hero and heroine in conflict, falling in love, retreating from love, going their separate ways, but somehow coming together by the end of the book. It was all so unreal. Life didn't always end happily-ever-after. C.B. knew that first hand. Love wasn't a pretty thing. In fact, love stung. It was too damn complicated, especially when it was dependent upon another person—a flawed and frightened person.

Good grief. Had her outlook about life changed so much in these months since the Daniel Episode? A year ago, she'd never have thought she would be so different. After all, she had believed in true love, in the happily-ever-after ending. She'd believed in Daniel. In their family. In their future.

"What's wrong?"

C.B. jerked up her head to find Jamie staring at her, sunlight throwing him into silhouette so that she couldn't see his face clearly. She hadn't even known she'd been crying. Quickly, she backhanded tears from her eyes with the palm of her hand.

"The book isn't that bad, is it?" There was humor in his voice mixed with genuine concern. Jamie stepped nearer.

"Oh, no!" She brushed more tears away. "I was only thinking about things."

"Sad things, it seems."

He sat across from her, something he rarely did. They'd kept their relationship professional. She liked it that way—or so she'd always told herself.

His expectant gaze caused her to glance away. He had the sexiest blue eyes for a man, even more appealing than Daniel's. And in his quiet way, he was more mature than Daniel. She liked his seriousness and his love of books and reading.

"Sometimes my mother would tell me her problems," he said softly. "She was divorced from my dad. Sometimes it helped her to get things off her chest."

"I have nothing to get off my chest," C.B. replied. Did he think she'd confide in him? "Some things make me sad, that's all."

"I know how it is," he said, musing. "I'm often sad."

Really, this was too much intimate information. This guy paid her to type manuscripts. Nothing more. C.B. gathered her self-respect around her, bolstered her courage. She was done with men—even ones who acted sympathetic and concerned. She would solve her own problems. She would make it on her own—well, with the help of her mom and dad. C.B. couldn't discount them when they had done so much for Scotty and her. In fact, without them, C.B.'s life would be one big piece of horseshit.

As if it wasn't anyway. As if she wasn't lonely most of the time. Angry and hurt, but mostly lonely.

Jamie sat back in his chair giving her breathing room. The table between them also provided protection, a physical barrier to prevent them from getting close. As the sun slid once more behind the clouds blocking the sun and throwing the room into shadows, he studied the bank of windows, not looking at her.

"Sometimes I get lonely," he said, staring up into space.

What? Did he really read her mind?

C.B. shook herself mentally, and to distract herself from his comment, she straightened the pile of papers on the table beside her laptop. "Well, life is a crapshoot, isn't it?"

His gaze returned to her, and he searched her face. "Yes, it certainly is."

As she'd hoped, her answer put him off, and he stood. Handing her another stack of handwritten papers, he gave her a sheepish grin. "I've brought you the first love scene to type."

Just what she wanted to read—a sex scene. She took the papers from him. "Thanks."

He seemed uncomfortable, suddenly terribly insecure. "You'll tell me what you think, won't you?"

He had never before asked for her opinion. Why now?

"Sure. If you want to hear it."

"I do. I care what you think, C.B. You are, in fact, my first reader and in the correct demographic."

Great. C.B. didn't want to be part of the lonely, female audience who escaped from an unhappy world through reading romance novels. But she was that woman, and he had recognized it.

She frowned up at him only to catch the gleam of humor in his eyes.

"Female," he said. "Twenty to forty. College educated. The right demographic."

He had been kidding her. Her frown deepened. She didn't get

him. Did he actually care what she thought? Maybe. Maybe not. But at that moment, she resolved to tell him exactly what was on her mind after she read his glorious, intellectual masterpiece.

~

"IT SUCKS."

Jamie lifted his pen, startled by C.B.'s quiet approach and by her harsh words. "It does?"

"Yes, it does."

"Thanks for the vote of confidence."

"Well, you wanted me to tell you what I thought."

But did she have to be so blunt? He liked honesty, but this smarted. He had felt uncertain of his effort because it was his first love scene without his mother's notes. In fact, the earlier two books for his publisher were simple rewrites of his mother's original drafts. He'd written the last one totally from her notes. This one was different. He was on his own with the new manuscript.

Jamie rose and shoved papers aside. He removed research books from the side chair. "Sit," he invited, "and tell me."

She alighted on the edge of the seat, favoring him with wide eyes and then bit her lip with nervous indecision. Her shyness didn't detract from her beauty but actually flattered her. C.B. was so damn cute, and she didn't even know it. What was the sizzle of attraction he continued to feel when around her? It was an unwelcome distraction. But in truth, he'd grown to love the morning when C.B. came to work. He'd come to depend upon her presence to cheer him up.

When she didn't speak, he inclined his head. "Go on."

"Well, it's like this." She hesitated. He nodded again, encouraging her. "There's no emotion," she said.

"There's not?"

"No. Just body part meeting body part."

"It's a love scene."

"Exactly. And it sounds like a man wrote it."

Jamie leaned back in his chair and studied her. A man *had* written it. What was it missing? Doubt assailed him. Maybe he couldn't do this, not well enough to satisfy his mother's readers. And if he couldn't do it, then the expensive nursing home that took such good care of his mother would be totally out of the question. He'd have to move her to a facility with fewer bells and whistles, and he hated that idea.

When he didn't respond immediately, C.B. shifted uneasily in her seat. "I don't read much romance," she confessed, "but the first book I typed, the one that had been published several years ago, was full of feelings. I could relate to the heroine—know what she was thinking during the love scene. This one...well...it is mechanical."

"I see." But did he? Fear of failure grabbed at his gut.

She looked self-consciously at him. "You wanted my opinion."

"Yes, but I need to figure out how to fix it." Jamie nodded and picked up the typed manuscript. The words looked better typed. Cleaner. Crisper. Mechanical.

"Put some emotion in it."

"Easier said than done," he said with a shrug. "I'm not a woman."

She glanced at him as if he'd grown an extra head. "But you're writing romance for women."

"Ironic, don't you think?"

"But you've captured the heroine's feelings before. What's different with this book?"

Now wasn't the moment for truth. He couldn't tell her about his mother and about him impersonating a famous writer. What if that news got out to the public? But he could reveal some of his own reality. Maybe that would stop her questions.

"It's been a long time since I've been in love," he admitted. "And I haven't had a date in ages."

"Well, take it from me, being in love isn't all that glamorous." She sounded bitter.

"Granted." He acknowledged her comment with a nod of his head. "But I'm a writer. I'm supposed to use my imagination."

At that moment, a sudden urge overtook him. What if he kissed C.B.? What if he got the feel again of a woman in his arms? It had been a long time since Julia, and he'd remained celibate since their break-up because he'd chosen to pursue his profession, study, and research and that caused him to live the life of a hermit. It was less complicated that way.

That stray urge swept through his body and almost doubled him over. Maybe if he practiced on his assistant, he could do a better job of describing the emotion she'd told him was lacking in the love scene.

Jamie asked her before he was aware the question left his mouth—almost as if an outside force directed his lips to form the words.

Her face flushed red. "What did you say?"

"I was wondering if you'd let me practice—just one kiss. I'd be doing research."

"That's the craziest line I've ever heard." She shot up from the chair and stared down at him. "I didn't agree to playing kissy face with you when I took this job."

Shame warmed his face. He climbed to his feet. "I know. I'm sorry. It was stupid of me to ask. A dumb idea."

"It certainly is!" C.B. turned and flounced from the room.

God, what an idiot. Jamie sank into his chair and picked up the manuscript. He read it again. Body part did join body part without one bit of emotion involved in the act.

Letting out a deep sigh, he pulled out a stack of ruled paper and started again, letting his cursive writing fill sheet after sheet. This time, he'd also let his imagination run wild and as he wrote, he pretended to make love to his lovely, but opinionated, assistant.

CHAPTER SEVEN

The next morning, Jamie flung open the front door before C.B. knocked. He shoved a sheaf of papers toward her. "I rewrote it," he announced, realizing he blatantly stared at the blue knit shirt that clung to her figure and outlined her full breasts.

"Okay. Well." C.B. seemed wary of his excitement or maybe she'd caught him ogling. She accepted the manuscript pages from him anyway. "Thanks."

"I switched point of view to the hero's," he said. "That way it was easier for me to capture the emotion you said was missing the first time."

He didn't reveal he'd created the love scene with her in mind. No, that wouldn't be such a good thing to disclose. To mix metaphors, rewriting those pages was like pulling hens' teeth. Delving into emotion he'd suppressed so long ago had dredged up a bunch of unwelcome heartache.

C.B. slanted him a suspicious glance and walked away. He kicked the door shut and followed her down the hall to the back porch where the April sun did its best to blind him. She dropped her shoulder bag on a chair and thumbed through his manuscript.

Finally looking up from the papers, she casually shrugged a shoulder. He released a breath he hadn't known he'd held. "What do you think?"

"So a medieval knight, the quintessential male chauvinist pig who thinks the only place a woman belongs is in the kitchen, barefoot and pregnant, is going to express these feelings when bedding his wife?"

"I prefer to call it making love—not bedding." He straightened his shoulders. Her reaction hurt. "It's what my readership expects."

"Fantasy," she said with a sneer.

"Fantasy," he echoed, "is what sells books."

She shrugged again as if it didn't matter to her. "Okay, I'll type it."

"That's what I pay you to do." He spoke too curtly.

She dropped her purse on the floor, sat down, and started to work, her fingers flying over the keyboard. He remained rooted in his spot. Silent. Deflated.

She stopped and looked up. "What?"

"Nothing." Spinning on his heel, Jamie retreated down the hall and escaped to his office.

His readers would like his changes, even though his assistant didn't. Jamie sank into his chair and dropped his head into his hands for a moment then picked up a pen and feverishly covered a blank page with his scrawling text. C.B. had made fun of his knight. Fine. He'd put in a dose of reality into the next scene and describe a battle full of blood and guts. If she wanted reality, he'd give it to her.

C.B. ENTERED JAMIE'S OFFICE—THE lion's den as she often thought of it—and stood near the door studying the lion. She'd quickly grown to appreciate her employer even though it was safer to act as if she could care less about him or his writing. He was a handsome man. Quiet. Thoughtful. Distinguished. The kind of man a woman could trust. But those kinds of thoughts were dangerous and C.B. knew it. She'd believed the same thing about Daniel. And look where that had gotten her.

He raised his head to discover her watching him. C.B. felt blood rise to heat her cheeks. Clearing her throat, she came toward his desk and handed him the typed manuscript pages. "It really is much better."

"Do you think so?"

He sounded relieved. He must have been genuinely distressed she'd dissed his love scene. Did all writers have such fragile egos?

"Yes, I think so. I can feel what the hero feels—his exuberance, his pride, his deepening love."

Jamie did a fist pump. "Yes!"

"Now you need to make the heroine less cookie-cutter. Give her some depth of emotion." C.B. sat down across the desk from him.

"As I said, that's easier said than done for me."

"Well, it shouldn't be. Your other books have it. You know, the old ones I've been typing."

"Yes, well…" He glanced away. "I've been told I have trouble expressing emotion."

She *had* upset him yesterday. She should have known. "I'm sorry I was so hard on you."

He looked back. "Oh, I don't mean by you."

She searched his face. Was he hiding something? Maybe it was what kept him closed up in this house, never going out, like a veritable recluse. A big part of her wanted to ask him who had hurt him, but she thought better of it. That was none of her business.

A beat of silence followed. C.B. drew a long breath.

"Why don't you come across the street to dinner tonight?" The idea bloomed as she said the words, a true spur of the moment whim. "It will just be me, Bekah, her kids, and my son Scotty. Maybe it will give you time to observe a couple of women." She paused and with a smile added, "Women in your right demographic. We might inspire you."

"Maybe more than you think," he said with a grin and then a shake of his head, "but I couldn't impose."

"You won't impose."

"But I couldn't."

Why was this man so frustrating? "Well, bring desert if it will make you feel better."

His eyes looked brighter, though wary. She was glad she'd made the offer. Now she needed to text Bekah to make sure there'd be enough to eat.

"Thank you, C.B. I'd be happy to have dinner with you tonight."

Why did his words sound so intimate? He made it sound as if the two of them were dining alone in a candlelit restaurant not in a kitchen with a passel of kids and her inquisitive housemate.

He favored her with a bashful smile, and she felt a thrill race down her spine. There was a developing connection between them. It embarrassed her. Troubled her. She didn't want to feel anything for another man, not after Daniel's betrayal. She couldn't trust herself to love like that again. She couldn't even chance an innocent attraction.

C.B. stood quickly, backing away from the desk and the man, and turning, she fled from the weird, erotic vibrations she had started to feel.

"I'd better get back to work," she called over her shoulder. "See you at six."

WHEN C.B'S GRANDMOTHER REMARRIED, she'd given the two-story, white frame house three blocks from the town square to

C.B.'s mother. Then her mother had married C.B.'s father, and they had turned the old house with its wraparound front porch and white picket fence into a bed and breakfast hotel. Keeping the original charm had been important to the family, so although they gutted the three upstairs bedrooms and attic to make suites and extra bathrooms for guests, they'd kept the front of the house and living room intact. But having a need for more dining space and a modern kitchen, C.B.'s parents had added on to the rear of the house creating an open-concept kitchen, dining, and sitting area.

At the moment, this kitchen dining room combination was the hub of pre-dinner activities. Fourteen-year-old Tara placed plates and cutlery on the table while her younger sister Courtney, sitting on the floor near a sofa, kept Scotty entertained with a set of giant Legos.

"You're more nervous than I've ever seen you," Bekah commented as she tossed a fresh green salad.

C.B. heard the humor in her friend's voice. "I know."

"We're entertaining a famous author," Bekah said, "or is there more to it?"

C.B. chose to ignore the last question. "Shhh! You're not supposed to know he's a famous novelist."

"Oh, my bad." More humor surfaced in Bekah's voice. "But I don't understand why he's so secretive. Why doesn't he want anyone to know?

"There's something about writing as a woman that has him spooked. He thinks if his readers find out he's a man, his sales will suffer."

"That's silly. I bet there's more to it than that. Maybe he's hiding a tragic love story."

C.B. didn't want to talk about Jamie, even though she'd thought about Bekah's speculations more than once. Time to change the subject. "So, should we have wine with the lasagna?"

"If we want to make an impression."

C.B. exhaled slowly. "Well, we do."

Bekah grinned at her and gave her an "I told you so" look. She nodded toward the wine rack. "I have a bottle of Pinot Noir. That's a good choice."

C.B. agreed and plucked the bottle of wine from the rack. She set out three stemmed, larger-bowled glasses on the table.

"Don't be so nervous," Bekah said again, looking up from removing the baking dish from the oven. "I can keep a secret. Besides, there's nothing wrong with being interested in him. Just because you're divorced doesn't mean you're dead."

C.B. felt defensive. Butterflies fluttered around in her stomach. "I don't know what you're talking about."

"Oh, don't you?"

The front doorbell sounded. "Saved by the bell."

C.B. marched into the living room. It was her turn to pause, catch her breath, and then fling open the door. Jamie stood on the porch smiling at her, his eyes expressing his delight. In his hands he held a plate of cookies covered with plastic wrap.

"For you," he said and extended the plate toward her. "You told me to bring dessert, and I knew you had kids. I made chocolate chip cookies from my mother's favorite recipe."

"Thank you." Why did she sound so breathless? "Won't you come in?" C.B. took the cookies from him, feeling those pesky butterflies swarm even faster.

Jamie entered the living room and his masculine presence filled the space. He wore navy-blue corduroy trousers and a gray sweater that emphasized his salt-and-pepper hair. Again she was impressed by his youthfulness, his trim physique, and smiling, cheerful attitude.

"I've always wondered about your B&B," he said looking around. "This is a charming room."

"My grandparents' house," C.B. explained. "My mom and dad remodeled it."

"Do you get many guests?"

"A fair amount. Tonight there's a retired couple staying here because they're in town to visit their grandchildren."

"Will they be here for supper?"

"No," C.B. said with a laugh. "We only do breakfast for the paying guests. The couple is at their daughter's house, I think. They mostly sleep here to have some privacy."

"Makes sense."

Small talk. But it put C.B. at ease, and she relaxed as Bekah burst into the room, drying her hands on a towel.

"Hello." Bekah extended a hand, not waiting to be introduced. "I'm Bekah Morgan, and I suppose you are our reclusive neighbor."

He blushed, bless his heart. C.B. smiled to herself.

"James Madison." Jamie shook Bekah's hand. "I work from home and don't get out much."

"C.B. said you were named after the president."

"Yes, one of my mother's little jokes."

The pleasantries continued into the kitchen and dining room area where the children were introduced. Tara and Courtney were polite but uninterested. Little Scotty, however, climbed up on Jamie's lap and sat there as if he belonged.

"Baptism under fire," Bekah whispered as she and C.B. plated the salads.

C.B. glanced at her son on Jamie's lap. "I suppose so." She didn't know what to think. Would Scotty intimidate this confirmed bachelor? Did it matter if he did? Scotty was her reality. There was no getting around that.

"No cell phones at the table," Bekah announced and was bombarded by teenage and pre-teen groans. "You know the rules."

C.B. removed Scotty from Jamie's lap and transferred him to his booster seat. The others gathered around the table and sat down. Bekah poured wine for the adults. They said a short prayer.

Jamie was the first to start conversation. "I suppose new technology is a curse and at times a godsend for children." He spooned lasagna onto his plate and then held the dish for C.B. so she could serve Scotty.

"Yes," Bekah said. "The girls played games on their devices early on. Now they mostly text or Snapchat with friends."

"Do you worry about cybersecurity?"

"Constantly. It's hard to keep up with all the recommended security measures, but I try."

"Bekah is a very good mother," C.B. chimed in. She didn't need to worry about cell phones just yet, even though Scotty had a tablet that wasn't connected to the Internet.

"And you are too," Bekah replied.

C.B. felt the flush spread to her cheeks. "We've had to be," she said, acknowledging Bekah. Her friend was a super single mom. She hoped she'd be half as good with her one son as Bekah was with her two girls.

WATCHING C.B.'S interaction with her son was eye opening. To see her as a loving, caring mom gave Jamie a new appreciation for her. How did she juggle a new job and raise a preschool-aged child too? She was a master at multitasking, for sure. C.B. reminded him of the qualities he'd appreciated about his mom, and he loved her all the more for it.

The stray thought walloped him hard, and he choked on a sip of wine, coughing as much to cover his surprise as to relieve the strangle reflex. Love? Where did that come from?

Concern popped into C.B.'s eyes. "Are you okay?"

"I inhaled when I should have swallowed." Jamie covered up the truth of his reaction.

"Well, be careful," she cautioned. "I'm fond of my job."

Their gazes met over Scotty's head, and Jamie felt like

choking again. She was so damn beautiful and so unaware of her charm. How could that ex-husband screw up their marriage so badly? If he were married to C.B., he'd love her and never let her go.

Love her. He toyed with the idea as the meal progressed. Did he love her? He hardly knew her. And he had no business succumbing to that tricky emotion, love. It was fantasy as C.B. had said. What gave him the right to think he had anything to offer a young woman like C.B.? Caring for his mother was a full-time responsibility. Besides, he'd made such a mess of things with Julia.

When dinner was over, the girls vanished to do homework—being excused to go across the open courtyard to their apartment in the first floor of the carriage house.

Jamie stood and picked up his plate and utensils. "Let me help with cleanup."

C.B. quickly shook her head. "Oh, no! You're company."

"I don't mind. Besides, a single mom raised me. I'm a pro when it comes to doing dishes."

Bekah gave them both a meaningful look as if she had something up her sleeve, as the idiom went. "How about you two cleaning the kitchen, and I'll get Scotty ready for bed?"

"Oh, no!" C.B. said again, letting alarm show on her face.

"C'mon," Bekah pleaded. "You have company, and I don't have a little one to read bedtime stories to any more."

C.B. glanced at Jamie. He could see the indecision and reluctance roll through her eyes. Silently, he urged her to accept Bekah's offer. He wanted more social time with her. When she conceded, he mentally jumped for joy then calmly marched to the country sink and started rinsing dishes to go into the dishwasher.

Later, when the kitchen was sparkling and ready for tomorrow's breakfast prep, they took the rest of the wine and two glasses out to the front porch swing and sat down. The night was filled with fragrant scents of spring and the cool air was pleasant.

Somewhere in the neighborhood, a dog barked. A car rumbled by on Main Street. Jamie poured a half glass of wine for each of them, finishing off the bottle, and placed it on the floor near the swing.

"It's such a nice night." Small talk. It filled the awkward silence between them.

"Yes." C.B. took a sip of wine.

Jamie pushed the swing with his feet, and it gently swayed. His shoulder touched C.B.'s and their thighs rubbed. His blood coursed, causing his heart to do double time. It was the most intimate, romantic time he'd spent on a porch swing in his thirty-some-years. Of course, that had to do with the woman beside him.

What was coming over him? God, he felt scared, but for the first time in ages…alive

"I know you're divorced," he said, probing for specifics, trying to find a topic of conversation. "Do you mind telling me what happened?"

She didn't say anything. He probably shouldn't have let his curiosity get the best of him and opened that can of worms.

"I don't want to bore you with the gory details," she finally whispered.

"I shouldn't have asked."

Quiet moments passed. C.B. breathed deeply and sipped her wine. Finally, she glanced at him and then looked away. "My father always says women divorce over money or another woman. In my case, it was another woman."

"I'm sorry."

"Plus I found out my husband wasn't the man I believed him to be."

"That's tough."

It *was* tough. Sounded like his mom. His no-good father had had another woman on the side too. The jerk had broken his

58

mother's heart. Jamie spent the rest of his childhood and now his adulthood trying to make it up to her.

Knowing what his mother went through gave Jamie a new appreciation for C.B. "No woman deserves to be left alone with a child to raise," he added.

C.B. tried to shrug off his comment. "It is what it is."

He wished he could alleviate her pain. The same ache in his throat surfaced that he experienced when he couldn't help his mom. And now he really couldn't help Jane Mallory Madison. He couldn't restore her health. All he could do was pay for her private care.

Gazing down at a stoic C.B., Jamie felt a rush of emotion. His attempts to draw her out, comfort her, were clumsy at best. He offered a weak smile and took her hand.

She stared at their clasped hands, not tugging away from his hold. "I never had a father growing up," C.B. told him in a breathless voice. "It was hard. I wanted a real family for Scotty."

Tears glistened in C.B.'s eyes. Jamie squeezed her hand. "Yeah, I hear you."

"All I ever wanted was to be part of a real family," she said again as if reiterating the thought would make it any less poignant. "With a mother and father and children."

He was with her. He understood. And he was near enough to see her pulse beating in her throat. Near enough to place a finger under her chin and lift it. Near enough to kiss her lips, gently at first, until her arms circled his neck and the gentleness turned to passion.

CHAPTER EIGHT

C.B.'s body caught fire. Despite the coolness of the night, her blood sizzled with awareness, desire, heartache—a myriad of emotions released when Jamie kissed her. She felt his desire, passion she hadn't felt from Daniel since the birth of Scotty—passion that might never have been present between her and her ex.

Jamie pulled her nearer, if that was possible, turning her toward him, and the swing rocked with their hunger. Then drawing away from her mouth, he kissed her throat, his breath warm and sensual. Her body tingled. Her breath quickened. His hand slipped to her outer thigh, and he stroked her leg that seemed to burn beneath the fabric of her blue jeans.

She wanted him. She wanted to strip off her clothes and have sex with him. She needed it. Needed the closeness—the fire of a long, slow release. His lips found her mouth, and she groaned as his kiss stunned her once more.

And then the noise of footfalls on the porch steps brought them up for air.

"Oh, pardon us," the male guest said. He held a key in his hand as he escorted his wife toward the front door.

C.B. and Jamie pulled apart. C.B. struggled to catch her breath, shame surging through her. What was she? A silly teenager caught in the act?

Jamie had the presence of mind to tell the couple the door was unlocked. They thanked him and hurried inside.

"That was awkward," he muttered, swiping a hand through his hair.

"But good practice," she countered. "Did you get what you needed for your book?"

"What?" He looked nonplused, as if uncertain what she meant.

"You needed research for your book."

Understanding, his eyes narrowed. "It wasn't for research. It just happened."

Great. And Daniel just happened to have an affair with that blond bimbo. She didn't say the cruel words, but he probably read her thoughts. She was sure her face was an open book.

He ran his hand through his hair again in a gesture of frustration. "That wasn't what I meant to say."

She sprang to her feet. She needed space. He was too near. Too vibrant. Too much a man. "Well, it just happened for me as well."

"I'm sorry, C.B." He got to his feet and went to where she stood near the front steps. "It wasn't very professional."

"No, it wasn't."

"But I can't say I didn't enjoy it."

She glared at him. "I bet you did."

Men. Were they all alike? She couldn't help but be wary of them. Of him. Of her strange and troubling feelings for this man who made her crave more.

"That didn't come out well either," he whispered.

"No, it didn't."

"You can see why love scenes give me trouble," he said with a self-deprecating laugh.

"Well, you had no trouble writing the one I typed today."

"No," he admitted. "No, I didn't."

He took a step nearer as if he wanted to kiss her again. His mouth slightly open, his eyes probed hers. C.B. felt a gravitational pull toward him. She swayed ever so slightly. He placed a hand on the support post and leaned forward.

Then his cell phone rang. He didn't ignore it and just let it ring. Standing upright, he slipped it from his pocket and glanced at it. "I need to take this."

"Sure." Sometimes she hated cell phones.

Jamie frowned and walked away from her to the end of the porch. With his back toward her, he answered his call. As she surveyed his broad shoulders, his sexy hips, and long, blue-jeaned clad legs, she heard his voice rise, but she couldn't make out his words. More mystery. C.B. swallowed hard. She was tired. She didn't need these mixed emotions.

He came back to her, almost as if he had a hat in his hands. Before he said a word, she could tell he needed something from her. Had she learned his mannerisms so well?

"What is it?"

Jamie inhaled a deep breath, glanced away, then back. "I need a favor from you."

"Figures. More practice?" She heard the bitterness in her voice.

"No." It was as if he had trouble putting his request into words. "Will you sit down?"

He sat down on the top step and patted the space beside him. What choice did she have? She needed his job. She didn't hate him. She was simply scared of what he made her feel.

C.B. sat down beside him. His body radiated warmth as her shoulder inadvertently rubbed his. He seemed troubled, almost in a panic.

"That was my agent," he explained.

"Okay."

"Another romance author had to cancel an engagement in

Lexington at the town's biggest independent bookstore, so my publisher wants me to take the slot instead."

"Okay."

"I don't want to do it." He sat forward, placing his head in his hands. "My agent says I must. It's written into my contract."

C.B. fought the urge to place an arm over his shoulder and give him a supporting hug. What was the big deal? And then it dawned on her.

"Your readers think you're a woman," she said softly.

He sat up and turned toward her. "You've got it." His eyes searched hers. There was something in them, an appreciation maybe or gratification that she understood. "The publisher has wanted me to do book signings for some time. My agent says I have to do them. Rob says I have to do them, but I've avoided them up to now."

"What are you going to do?"

He didn't miss a heartbeat with his response. "Will you pretend to be me?"

"What?"

"Will you take my place? I'll come with you, of course, sit beside you at the signing, pretend to be your boyfriend in case you get questions you can't answer. You can sign 'Madison Mallory' as well as I can. It's a pseudonym, after all."

"But it's a lie!"

"So is my pen name."

She couldn't believe he was asking her to lie. She hated lies. Maybe because of Daniel. Maybe because her mother had spanked her as a child when she told a story and then lied to her about the identity of her father. Whatever it was, C.B. didn't like it. She didn't want to be part of Jamie's falsehood.

He must have understood. Good grief. Was she that easy to read?

He clutched her hand. "I know you don't want to do it."

"You think?" She looked down at his hand, and he removed it as if her gaze burned through his skin.

He looked away. She sensed his struggle. "The truth is," he said with a sigh, "I must fulfill my contract or your father says I can be sued. I need this contract because I need the money. It's not just for me. Other people depend upon me."

"We all have our issues." She didn't want to give him an inch.

"If readers find out a man is behind Madison Mallory, I'm afraid my readership will fall off. If that happens, my royalties will suck." He turned to her, his eyes insistent. "C.B., I need your help. Will you help me?"

In the past, when Daniel asked her to do something, she'd acquiesce without hesitation. He had been her husband, after all. It was her place to support him. Do for him. Love him. But where had that kind of devotion gotten her? Surely, Jamie's request was different. What was he to her? Nothing more than an employer, one who when the manuscripts were typed would no longer need her services. Just because some part of her lusted for him didn't mean she couldn't control those feelings. And it didn't mean she had to do what he said if she was uncomfortable with it.

No, she didn't have to lie for him. She wouldn't lie for him.

But the more he silently pleaded with his eyes, and the more she searched his face, her resistance crumbled.

"Okay, I'll do it, but against my better judgment."

"Oh, I could kiss you!"

"We've done that, thank you very much." She climbed to her feet and crossed the floor to pick up the glasses and empty bottle.

He stood up too, looking penitent, humble, and good enough to kiss again. Gosh, she had to get that image out of her mind.

"I really appreciate this, C.B."

"Consider it part of my job." She would not make any concessions. "When is this book signing?"

He paused and scuffed his toe. "Tomorrow. Three o'clock."

"You're kidding?"

"As serious as sin."

His grin caught her off guard. "What if I'd said no?"

He shrugged. "I had faith you wouldn't."

"Wonderful." Was this man for real? And was she that much of a pushover? "I'll be late to work tomorrow, because I'll need to get Scotty settled in with my mom. I may as well ask her to keep him overnight."

"You'll be at my house before noon? We'll need to leave by then."

"Don't worry. You have my word."

"Thank you, C.B." He took a step toward her.

She backed away. "Mallory, remember?"

"Mallory, it is." He smiled at her, and she thought her insides would burn. "I'll see you tomorrow, Mallory Madison."

"Sure."

"Thanks for dinner."

"Sure."

As he left her, crossing the street and letting himself into his house, C.B. felt her heart fill up like a balloon. Was she making a mistake? What was she getting herself into? Some part of her felt as if this was a disaster ready to happen. Another part thought she had started on a new path, and for whatever reason, she'd follow it until something happened to burst that flimsy balloon.

CHAPTER NINE

Kelly watched her daughter unload Scotty from his car seat. Her grandson sprinted across the driveway toward her open arms, and she gave him huge hug. Then Kelly led Scotty into the house holding his hand.

"Thanks for doing this, Mom," C.B. carried Scotty's duffle bag with her and followed Kelly inside.

"You know I don't mind helping out."

"Since I started working, I've asked for your help a lot more." C.B. sounded defensive. She dropped the bag on the sofa. "I brought his blanket and pajamas. Make sure he brushes his teeth before bed."

"I know the drill." Kelly surveyed her daughter, who was dressed in a blue, two-piece pantsuit. "What's going on today?"

C.B. averted her gaze and shifted her stance. "Mr. Madison has asked for my help in Lexington. I thought I'd better look the part. I don't want to disappoint him."

"Well, you look beautiful."

C.B. smiled. "You're a bit prejudiced, Mom."

"Guilty! I'm a proud mother, you know?"

C.B. blushed and busied herself settling Scotty in with his

wooden blocks and toy trains. Her daughter reminded her so much of herself—overprotective and sensitive. How Kelly had loved the little girl she'd given birth to so many years earlier. Now her baby had a baby of her own. It was gratifying, to say the least.

But something was going on with her daughter, even though C.B. wouldn't own up to it. Just as a mother's sixth sense told her when something was wrong, Kelly knew C.B. well enough to see a faint change in her mood. If asked, she wasn't sure she could explain the difference to Rob. Was it a lighter step? A subtle glow? She couldn't remember the last time C.B. had dressed up like this. The part-time job certainly had been good for her.

Kelly paused and sharply scrutinized her daughter. Unless... Could it be? She hoped C.B. had learned from her past mistakes, because the more she thought about it, the more Kelly was convinced it wasn't simply work that had buoyed C.B.'s spirits.

It was *someone*.

THE SIGNING TOOK place in a store located at a prominent Lexington mall. Its two floors also contained sections of local gifts, handcrafted art, children's toys, and a mix of audiobooks, DVDs, and even CDs. The romance section was extensive, filled with paperbacks and hardbacks. An endcap displayed an assortment of Madison Mallory historical romances.

C.B. had loved the smell of books since library visits as a child. Stacks of books, row after row of them, had caught her imagination then, and she'd become an avid reader. Today's modern bookstore contained a different ambiance with the aroma of coffee and the scent of candles. Nevertheless, the new smells couldn't mask the comfortable odor of books.

"You doing okay?" Jamie asked as the shop manager showed

them to the table set up for them near a group of comfy sofas on the second floor.

"Sure."

Why wouldn't she be okay? She was about to lie to people. All night she'd second-guessed herself, wondering why she'd agreed to this deception.

In the cruel light of the new day, she regretted her tendency to want to please the people in her life—especially men.

"I appreciate you doing this." Jamie wouldn't let it go.

"It's my job."

"I still appreciate it."

"No problem."

C.B. fought down the churning in her stomach and took a seat at a table covered with a white cloth and stacked with Madison Mallory books. A basket of candy kisses had been left on the table along with a bottle of water. C.B. selected a candy, unwrapped the silver wrapping, and popped the treat into her mouth, savoring the chocolate.

"I'll announce your arrival over the PA system," the manager told them and headed to the escalator.

C.B. turned to Jamie. "Now what?"

"We wait and see if anyone shows up." He ran a jerky hand through his hair then gave her a halfhearted grin. "Relax. Let me be nervous for both of us."

Her return smile wavered. Relax, he said. Would she be able to pull off the deception? For a moment, she could only stare back at him, at the anxious flicker in his eyes. Memory of last night's kiss tightened her chest. She looked away.

Jamie was unsure of himself...vulnerable. She'd never thought of Daniel as vulnerable until the last moment when he was lying on the pavement begging her not to call the cops. Something that was so unappealing in Daniel gave Jamie a fascinating charm. How was she supposed to react to that paradox?

"We'd like to welcome the famous romance writer Madison

Mallory to our store." The announcement came over the store speaker system. "Please join us upstairs where she is signing her newest Scottish clan novel."

"Here we go," Jamie said.

But nothing happened. No one stopped by their table for a good twenty minutes, but finally a few fans began to trickle in one or two at a time. It wasn't a steady stream, but C.B. played her part well, signed books, smiled, and chitchatted with readers. When she didn't know an answer to a question, Jamie was quick with it. He'd been right about one thing. Women made up Mallory Madison's audience.

An hour into the event, a heavy-set woman approached the table. She wore a blue, University of Kentucky sweatshirt and jeans and carried a shopping bag filled with well-worn paperbacks.

"I hope it's okay, honey, to bring all my books for you to sign?" The fan leaned over the table. "I've loved your books for years. You write the sexiest heroes."

"Oh, thank you very much." C.B. pasted a smile upon her face and held up her pen with purple ink. "I'll be glad to sign anything you want."

The woman carefully stacked seven books on the table. "I want your new book, of course."

"Should I make the dedication to you?"

"Make them all to Gloria, honey, if you please." She spelled her name.

C.B. composed different dedications, then scrawled the signature of Madison Mallory on the fly leaf of each book.

"This one has to be my favorite," Gloria said, handing C.B. the last book in the bag, a worn paperback entitled *Lord of the Mist*. "I was only fifteen when I bought it."

The book was thick—at least five hundred and fifty pages with tiny print.

"Those were the days," the lady said wistfully. "A body could lose herself in a big book like this. Books are too short these days."

C.B. flipped to the copyright page. It had been published in 1978. She turned one more page and signed "Best Wishes to my biggest fan, Madison Mallory."

After the woman had collected her books and departed, C.B. sat back in her chair. She removed the cap from the bottled water and took a sip. Her stomach tensed with suspicion. Something wasn't right. How could Jamie publish a book in 1978? She whipped her head around toward him.

A bemused smile tugged at the corner of his lips. "What?"

"How old you are? You never told me."

"Thirty-seven. Why?"

C.B. screwed the cap back on the bottle and set it aside. How quickly had another man had burst her balloon? She felt deflated as if Daniel's beat-up motorbike had once more crashed into her car. "So you were born in 1980?"

"That's right."

"Then how did you manage to write a book before you were even a gleam in your parents' eyes?"

SHE'D CAUGHT HIM. Jamie opened his mouth then shut it. What could he say?

C.B. said it for him. "I told you I don't like deceiving people."

"I can explain."

"Don't bother."

She wouldn't talk to him. Or look at him. He felt his chest tighten at the cold shoulder she gave him. Sitting back, Jamie watched another reader approach. C.B. signed the book. Her smile was now strained and her eyes dull with disillusionment.

He didn't want to be the cause of her disappointment. It

wasn't the way he'd been raised. Besides, she'd become important to him in more ways than one.

After the event was over, they walked to the car not saying a word. "Do you want to go to dinner?"

"No," she said. "I want to go home."

More silent treatment. He couldn't let this continue. He owed her an explanation. The simplest way to explain was to show her. Jamie put the car in gear and drove to his mother's nursing home.

Questions popped into C.B.'s eyes once he parked the car. "I want to introduce you to someone," he said.

She opened her mouth to object.

"Please?"

In a huff, C.B. climbed out of the passenger side and shadowed him into the home. As clean and pleasant as the staff tried to make the facility, it remained a nursing home. The wide, linoleum halls were flanked with grab bars and railings. A couple of empty wheelchairs sat idly at the nurses' station. The antiseptic smell couldn't quite cover a stronger one of sadness, fear, and old age.

"I wasn't expecting you today, Mr. Madison," a nurse behind the counter said.

"Spur of the moment, Hannah," he replied with a nod. "Is my mother in her room?"

"No, she's in the living room waiting for dinner."

"Thank you." Jamie took hold of C.B.'s elbow and guided her down the hall. She felt stiff, hostile, but curiosity lit her eyes.

"Jamie, what's this?" she asked quietly.

"I want you to meet my mother."

Turning to look at C.B., he interpreted her questions and gave a sad smile. She was so beautiful. She'd been through so much in her short life and he wanted to reach out and protect her. He wanted to kiss her again too. His face flushed as his mind spun through the ramifications of what he was feeling.

They found his mother sitting by herself in a wheelchair near a sunny window. Her eyes were vacant. Her lips formed silent words. In her hands, she held a crocheted potholder as if she had been working on it. She wore a flowered housecoat over a loose-fitting dress. When they approached, she looked up and smiled.

Jamie took her hand. She stared at it a moment then glanced at him and smiled again.

"Jane Mallory Madison," he said, misery choking his throat. "I'd like to introduce you to my friend Colleen Lyons."

"Pleased to meet you," his mother said, turning her blank gaze from Jamie to C.B.

"I'm pleased to meet you too, Mrs. Madison." C.B. touched the older woman's hand.

"We won't stay long, Mom," Jamie said. "You're going to have dinner soon."

His mother stared through him. "Have you seen James? My son? I thought he might visit me today."

Jamie's heart broke for the hundredth time. "I'm James, Mom."

Mrs. Madison turned to C.B. "Do you know my son? He's a good boy."

"Yes, ma'am, I believe he is."

CHAPTER TEN

It was as if a balloon once again filled C.B.'s chest with air. With its expansion came a deep understanding. Jamie's mother was the real Madison Mallory.

The woman in the wheelchair didn't look old, but her world obviously had been stripped from her by some sort of dementia. It didn't seem fair. But life wasn't fair.

Heavens! Poor Jamie. He must be living in hell. C.B.'s throat ached with compassion, and more than that...a sudden burst of love.

Sick with the revelation, C.B. bit her lip, fighting back tears. As she stood rigidly apart from mother and son, C.B. watched the tableau in front of her and grappled with her newfound emotion. She couldn't be in love with Jamie. He was older by a good ten years and a confirmed bachelor.

But that wasn't the crux of the problem. *She* was. Her history of neediness and picking the wrong man was the problem. Whenever she loved, she gave herself up and let her identity yield to the man's. She became what he wanted. Compliant. A submissive shell of herself.

No. She could not go through that misery again.

But how could she ignore the fluttering in her chest? And seeing the gentle way Jamie treated his mother, C.B. couldn't disregard what she was feeling. Was he as goodhearted as he seemed? Would it be safe to care for him just a little?

"I suppose you have a ton of questions," he said a few minutes later as they walked to the car.

"Your mother is obviously the real Madison Mallory."

"Yes." He opened the passenger-side door for her.

"She doesn't know you, does she?"

"No. Not any more."

Holding the door, Jamie was inches away, so near she sensed his sadness. He looked at her lovingly, pausing, and his gaze dropped to her mouth. His eyes darkened. In that moment, she failed to breathe. The wind lifted a tendril of her hair, and he smoothed it away from her face. Her traitorous body tilted toward him. She wanted to kiss him. Why had she suddenly become powerless where he was concerned?

"No," she cried in a halting voice and twisted away from him. If she kissed him, she risked losing herself again. She slid into the car seat instead.

He shut her door and came around to join her in the car. "It's okay, C.B.," he said. "It really is okay."

"Jamie, I'm so sorry." For many things. Not just his mother.

"I owe you an explanation." He started the car and pulled out of the parking lot. "The only way I have enough money for a good nursing facility is if Madison Mallory continues to sell books."

"I see." Everything made sense. C.B. had to applaud him for his initiative. It was so heartbreaking though.

"Do you understand now why I kept it a secret?"

"After meeting Madison Mallory's readers, yes."

He nodded, but directed his eyes toward the road. Glancing over at him, C.B. saw the set of his jaw and the look of resignation in his eyes. He was such a handsome man with his graying hair and blue eyes. There was a sincerity and kindheartedness about him she'd never seen in Daniel.

"Thank you for trusting me with the information," she finally said.

"You needed to know."

"You're doing a noble thing."

"No. I'm doing what I have to do."

C.B. DIDN'T WANT to stop for dinner so he drove her straight back to Heritage Springs. He parked in his alley parking spot, and they entered his house through the sunroom. He flipped on the lights, and the room glowed brightly, cutting through the gloom Jamie had felt during the drive. C.B. had been quiet. Too quiet. Had she misinterpreted his urge to kiss her? Was she mad at him for that or something more?

"I don't know about you," he said striding into the kitchen, "but I'm hungry. I believe I have salad fixings in the refrigerator."

She followed him into the kitchen. "I'll just go home."

He opened the refrigerator door and turned to give her a smile. "Why? If I remember, your mother is babysitting."

She didn't deny it but failed to return his smile. Jamie shut the refrigerator door and crossed the floor to where she stood. "C.B., what's wrong?"

Searching his face, she shook her head ever so slightly. Tears welled in her eyes. "It's so sad."

Ambushed by fresh pain, he nodded. His mother's life had been cut short, as she'd feared would happen three years ago when she urged him to take over her books. The illness progressed fast. It was hard to visit her, understanding she did not know him. "My mother is not in pain," he told C.B. "She's happy in her own way, I think."

"It's so unfair."

There was nothing he hated more than a woman's tears. "Don't cry, C.B."

She swiped a hand across her eyes. "I can't help it." Then she gave him a watery smile, fighting to control her emotions.

He'd never wanted a woman so much in his life. And that scared him. "Oh, God, C.B. Don't cry."

"It's not only your mother."

"I know." And he did know. She was suffering still from the trauma of her divorce. He'd been through it in a lesser fashion with Julia and had held himself aloof from his emotions for many years. But there was something about this woman that drew him.

He stepped forward and took her into his arms, hugging her close. C.B.'s sobs came swiftly then as one human sought to comfort another. His brain screamed warnings, but his body betrayed him. He kissed the top of her head, inhaling the scent of her hair and her sweetness. He wanted her with every fiber of his being so threw away all caution. Would she have him? Was he a fool to ask?

"I want you," he whispered, "as a man wants a woman."

"Research?" She didn't pull away.

"Hell, no. I want to be with you, because I love you."

C.B. wiggled in his arms as if to break free, but he wouldn't release her. "There's no future for us," she said. "Not with Scotty. I can't do that to him."

"I don't care about a future." And he didn't. Not now. In recent days, he'd learned to live in the moment. "I need you now, C.B. Tomorrow will take care of itself."

She lifted her head, and he saw her tearstained eyes. She shook her head ever so slightly.

"Can't two humans comfort each other?" he asked. "We need each other tonight. Let me make love to you, C.B. I'll expect no commitment."

Something told him he wanted more from her than one night, but the moment weighed heavily on him. Her lips were so inviting. Her sadness so compelling. If he could help her forget, he would do so even if it were a temporary fix. What guarantee did human beings have? Only now. Only the instant.

When he kissed her lips, Jamie allowed his pent-up emotions to surface. All his past longings, his heartache, and his desires poured into that one kiss. It swept them away. Blew them away. Brought them together.

"Tonight," C.B. murmured. "I'll give you tonight."

"That's enough."

He moved back and took her hand, drawing her down the darkened hallway toward the staircase to the second floor. Pausing at the foot of the steps, Jamie stifled a self-conscious laugh.

"What?"

"Something compels me to make a grand gesture," he told her, looking down and capturing her with his smile. "Like in a romance novel."

"What are you going to do? Carry me up the stairs?"

He laughed. "If I can."

And so he scooped C.B. off her feet and into his arms. What was he thinking? The climb up to the second floor was more of a struggle than a magnificent act of drama, but it broke the ice. They giggled all the way to the top, and when Jamie set C.B. on her feet by his bed, she looked at him and said simply, "You are my hero."

CHAPTER ELEVEN

With the dawn, C.B. regretted the previous night. She turned her head to the side to see Jamie asleep beside her in a jumble of sheets and pillows. God, what had she done? Would she be able to face him in the cold morning light?

They'd done the deed. Made love. And it had felt, at the time, as if they had actually been in love. She'd come quickly and that had surprised her. Even with protection, she'd been ready for release. But was that because she was young and had been without a man for so many months?

Or had it anything to do with feelings for Jamie?

She didn't want to have feelings for him. Hadn't she warned herself yesterday about the consequences of falling in love with another man? She couldn't make that mistake again.

C.B. looked away from Jamie and stared at the open bedroom door. They hadn't even taken time to shut it. Her dressy pants and jacket, bra and panties were crumpled on the wooden floor near the bed. This simply didn't feel right. She wasn't a one-night-stand kind of girl. She wanted to be in a relationship for the long haul not just indulge in a transient affair.

Rolling over on her side away from him, C.B. knew this wouldn't work. Jamie wasn't in this for anything more than a short-term thing. He'd said so, hadn't he?

When she made a move to leave the bed, Jamie draped an arm over her shoulder, pulling her back. "Don't leave," he said in a sleepy voice. "Stay with me, please?"

She turned into his arms. What did she want? If she stayed was she giving up herself again? Or did she want to be with him? For this morning…until it was time to pick up Scotty? What did she want?

Lifting a fingertip to stroke his beard-roughened jaw, C.B. surrendered again.

For the moment.

LATER THAT SUNDAY AFTERNOON, the weather was crisp with plenty of sunshine, blue sky, and wispy clouds. C.B. joined Scotty, her mom and dad and grandparents at The Eagle's Nest Grist Mill and restaurant for an early evening dinner of fried fish, fries, hush puppies, and coleslaw. It was one of C.B.'s favorite meals. Maybe because Scotty loved eating here and playing near the fishponds. Whatever it was that made this place so special, she was glad to be with her family. Hers might have been, at times, dysfunctional and cobbled together in the past few years, but it remained a happy, loving family. She couldn't escape the thought that Jamie didn't have one. And that made her sad.

After dinner, Rob, Kelly, and her grandfather Howie, followed Scotty around the first of two ponds as the little boy explored along its banks. C.B. and her grandmother Grace stopped beside the mill trace and listened to the slap-slap sound of the water-powered paddle.

"Let's sit and relax," Grace said, sitting down on a wooden bench nearby.

After the emotional rollercoaster ride of the previous day and night, C.B. was glad to take up her grandmother's offer. They sat quietly a few minutes, soaking in the sun and listening to the distant laughter of children.

"So, Colleen, dear, what's the matter?"

C.B.'s head snapped around. She stared into the wise eyes of her grandmother. "What do you mean?"

"I watched you at dinner. There's something wrong."

C.B. averted her gaze. "There's nothing wrong, Gran."

"Why don't I believe you?"

C.B. squeezed her eyes shut a moment. Doggone it. Her grandmother was too perceptive.

Grace's voice filled with regret. "I'm sorry we don't seem to be able to talk to each other anymore."

Turning back, C.B. reached out and touched her grandmother's sleeve. "It's not your fault, Gran," she whispered. "I've just been going through a lot these past months."

"All the reason to talk to your old granny."

"You're not old," C.B. scoffed.

Grace grinned, her gaze drifting across the pond to where her husband strolled with Rob and Kelly. "I don't feel old."

"Well, you're not."

"Howie gave me a new lease on life," she said.

C.B. tamped down a flicker of envy. She was happy for Grace, she really was. It had taken her grandmother a lifetime to find such happiness. She prayed it wouldn't take her as long.

"I sometimes wish I had what you and Howie have," C.B. admitted.

"You'll find it when the time is right."

C.B. frowned. "That's just it. How do you know when the time is right?"

Grace laughed a little. "You don't know."

"Wonderful." C.B. suspected that was the way it would be.

JAN SCARBROUGH

"Sometimes you simply must take a leap of faith," Grace divulged.

"Is that what you did with Howie?"

Grace paused a beat, using that time to study her granddaughter. "Yes. After I realized I was a better person with Howie than without him."

C.B. tilted back her head to study the sky. A sense of despair washed over her. She lowered her head and turned to her grandmother. "I felt that with Daniel," she said, "but I was lying to myself."

It was Grace's turn to reach out a comforting hand and place it on C.B.'s. "Have you found someone new?"

Had she? Memories of making love with Jamie flooded into her consciousness. C.B. felt her face grow warm. It had been so good with him. He'd acted as if he loved her. But what was she to believe?

Grace squeezed her hand. "You don't need to tell me, dear."

"I'm not ready, Gran."

"I understand." Grace withdrew her hand and brushed a strand of gray hair from her eyes. "Do you remember what you told me the day you married Daniel?"

C.B. shook her had. How could she remember that day? Her insides ached with grief—for the marriage that failed and the man she'd once loved.

Having circled the fishing pond, the rest of the family approached where they sat.

Grace leaned nearer so they wouldn't hear. "You told me that it is never too late to find true love. Howard told me that too. I was in my sixties when I met Howie. I didn't believe him." She patted C.B.'s hand. "Have faith, Colleen."

Grace rose and went to meet her husband. C.B. choked back tears as she watched them hold hands like teenagers. Her mother and father had found each other again after twenty years. The

84

two couples were role models. She'd do well to remember their examples.

However, she wasn't sure she had the courage of the women who went before her. She wasn't sure if she could take that leap of faith when the time came to make the big jump.

CHAPTER TWELVE

To say the least, Monday morning was awkward. Jamie met C.B. at the door as usual. His mind had been adrift all the previous day and night. Now that she was with him again, he was back to normal. His mind was clear—his head on straight.

"I thought about you all night," he admitted as she entered the hallway.

She blushed prettily and hid her eyes. C.B. looked about as awkward as he felt. Did that mean she'd thought about him too? Did it mean she didn't regret their time together?

She lifted her head and caught him staring. "I'd better get busy so you can pay the bills."

He stepped aside. "By all means."

She strode past him with purpose, heading straight into the sunroom and her desk. He followed her and stood silently watching from the doorway as she started to type. Why couldn't he think of a damn thing to say? Why did he feel like a bumbling ass?

Returning to his office, he couldn't concentrate. Maybe his head wasn't on straight after all. Their night together had taught him how lonely he had been all these years. After C.B. had left, he'd realized how much life she brought to his house—to him. Unlike with Julia, he hadn't experienced any trouble feeling emotion with C.B. In fact, he felt overcome with it—needy, desperate to please her, to make her happy. He wanted to rush into the sunroom right now and take her into his arms, lift her up, and carry her to bed. He wanted to ravish her as if he were one of his romance novel heroes. He wanted to make love to her. Again. And again. Forever.

Instead, he slowly walked back into the sunroom and dropped a house key on the desk near her computer.

She surveyed him through shadowed lashes. "What's this?"

"The key to the front door." He paused, unsure of what to say. "I thought you might use it if you get free time, and I'm not home."

"Okay, thanks." She pocketed the key, glanced back at the keyboard, and then back at him.

"I don't know what to say," he murmured.

"Don't say anything."

How could he express what he really felt? He reached out to touch her cheek. She flinched.

"Don't."

That hurt—deep down where his stone-cold heart supposedly beat.

"I'm sorry," he said.

"Don't be." She was curt. "I'm a grown woman. I made my own decision."

It sounded so terse. Brusque. As if they had experienced no emotional connection between them. He didn't believe it. C.B. just didn't want to face their growing bond. Because he knew of her past, he tried to understand. He tried to think it was something he could overcome if he gave it enough time.

"Good," he said and backed away. "I'll let you get to work."

Leaving was the hardest thing he'd ever done.

~

C.B. HAD TROUBLE CONCENTRATING. That Jamie was only a room away made her stomach flutter. Knowing what they'd done upstairs filled her head with cobwebs. Maybe if she refused to engage in conversation, she could make it through the day. She let lunch pass without taking it with Jamie as usual. By the time it was two o'clock, when her stomach rumbled with hunger, she realized she needed a break.

Going to the kitchen, she poured herself a glass of tea and squeezed a lemon over the iced drink. She stirred the beverage slowly, reliving things her grandmother had said. Was Jamie really someone new?

And then her cell phone rang in her pocket. She drew it out of her jeans, saw the caller was her father, and accepted the call.

"C.B.?"

"Yes, Dad."

"Can you come over to my office?"

"Sure. When?"

"Now if you can get away."

Was something wrong? She steeled her shoulders, disregarding the fear in her stomach. "I need to pick up Scotty at daycare."

"No need. Your mom has gone to get him. If she needs to, she'll feed him his supper."

"You're scaring me, Dad."

He didn't answer right away. "I don't think you'll be happy with my news. That's why I want you to come to my office."

"Sure." She lowered the cell phone and clicked off.

"Is something wrong?"

Jamie was there in the room, concern written in his eyes. He looked so good. So steady. She longed to run to him, to have him make whatever it was go away. But she remained impassive. Stoic.

"My father has news for me, and I'm to come to his office now."

"Sounds serious. Want me to go with you."

His offer caught her off guard. "No. I'll handle it."

"I'll be glad to go with you."

"I said no!"

C.B. turned away. Good grief. She didn't mean to yell, but he wasn't anything to her, just a one-night stand. She couldn't depend upon him. Didn't need him. The only person she could rely upon was herself—and her family. They never wavered.

"I'm sorry," she said, turning back to face him.

Jamie was by her side her then. He held her upper arms, drawing her close even though she resisted. He kissed her hair and whispered, "It will be okay. I'm here if you need me."

That's just it. She didn't want to need him. She didn't want to feel as if all she wanted to do was fold into his embrace and stay with him, comfortable and cozy forever.

"WHAT'S WRONG, DAD?" C.B. entered her father's office prepared to do battle.

"Sit down."

C.B. sat down hard in a chair across the desk from her father. The knots in her stomach twisted tighter. "Tell me," she urged.

Rob sat back in his chair. "Daniel is out of rehab. He's satisfied the court that he's clean."

Daniel? She didn't care about Daniel. They were divorced. "Good for him."

Her father cleared his throat. "That means he's eligible for limited visitation with Scotty."

"What?" C.B. sat forward in the chair and gripped its wooden arms. "That scumbag isn't going to see my son."

Rob shook his head as if to tell her she was wrong. "He's the boy's father. He has his rights."

"I won't have it!"

"You have no choice, C.B."

A huge wave of panic flowed through C.B. She fought to breathe. "Daniel is a danger to himself and others. I won't let him see Scotty," she hissed.

The lawyer in her father surfaced. He was calm. Quiet. "Daniel will be given the chance to visit with Scotty every week. First, his parents must be present to supervise his visits. Later, if he proves himself stable and stays out of trouble, he will be granted longer visits. We may eventually renegotiate extended visits where Daniel can take Scotty to Louisville for a weekend."

"No!" C.B. jumped up and paced the room. "I won't allow it."

"You have no choice," Rob repeated.

She would run away with her son. There was no way that double-dealing bastard would get his hands on her boy. No way!

Terror rose in her throat. This couldn't be happening? Hadn't seeing her husband with that skanky blond bimbo been bad enough? Now she was being forced to give up her son.

"Daniel's parents are bringing him to town tomorrow. I can drive Scotty to the Eagle's Nest to meet them. You don't have to go, and you don't have to see him."

C.B. stopped and stared at her father. "Why the Eagle's Nest?"

"We thought that would be a good spot to meet because it's a place Scotty knows and likes. We felt he'd be comfortable there. Besides, it's a public place."

"We?" C.B. balled her fist and rested them on her hips. "You planned this without me?"

"Your mother and I thought we'd spare you the heartache."

"I live with the heartache." Her answer dripped with sarcasm.

She prowled the law office, biting back her anger. Scotty was her son. Her parents meant well, but this was her enemy to conquer. If Scotty had to see his father, she'd do it.

"I'll take Scotty tomorrow," she said, knowing full well it would be one of the hardest things she'd ever do.

~

AFTER SHE LEFT her father's office, C.B. had a couple hours reprieve before picking up Scotty at her parents' house. God, what would she have done without them? She hated to think about trying to get through this divorce on her own.

Rain had come from the west. The weather was damp and the day had turned gloomy—as gloomy as her mood. She drove around the square, and almost as if her car had a mind of its own, she headed toward the B&B. But she didn't stop on the street in front of the house. She drove instead to the alley across the street and parked at Jamie's back door. His car was in its usual spot. A light burned in the kitchen. He was home.

Fingering his house key in her pocket, C.B. sat back and stared at the dark sunroom.

Should she go away? Turn on the ignition and back out into the alley? Why did her insides ache to be with Jamie? What was this scary compulsion?

Before she could act, he opened the back door. Jamie stood in the doorway watching her. His eyes seemed to devour her even from the distance as if pleading for...what?

Knowing she'd lost this battle, C.B. slowly climbed out of her car and walked across the patio. One step. Two. Then she was in his arms, sobbing, holding tightly to his neck, feeling the thud of his heart and the shower of kisses on her hair, her cheeks, her neck.

"Oh, God, Jamie."

She could think of nothing more to say. He drew her into the house as the rain started to fall again.

"What's wrong, C.B.? Is it Scotty? Your parents?"

Her answer was lost in his kiss. She sensed his vitality. His heat. His desire. Breathing in ragged gasps, C.B. felt her body ready to explode.

"C.B.," he said with a moan of acceptance. "Tell me what is wrong."

All the way down the hall and up the steps to Jamie's bedroom, they scattered clothing along their path, and C.B. told him about tomorrow and Scotty, and why the man she had once loved was tearing her soul from her body.

CHAPTER THIRTEEN

C.B. arrived at the mill and restaurant early the next day, thinking she'd let Scotty play on the playground and settle in. She wished she could settle in—calm the nerves that ran rampant through her stomach making her feel nauseous. Instead, she gritted her teeth as she pushed Scotty in a swing and tried to relax her tight muscles. She would soon see Daniel for the first time in ten months. How would he act? How would she respond?

Minutes later, the Lyons' Porsche Cayenne stopped at a parking space by the main building. It was time. Her cell phone buzzed. C.B. swallowed with difficulty and answered. Mr. Lyons asked her location. She told him, watched him climb out of his car, look her way, and wave. She waved back.

Then she slowed the swing to a halt and knelt down in front of Scotty. "Your daddy is coming to see you," she told her little boy, who stared back wide-eyed, his flaxen hair tousled by wind. "Give him a hug, okay? He's missed you."

The little guy nodded and took her offered hand. Together they walked from the grass and sawdust of the play area to the paved pathway that circled the stocked fishponds. As the trio drew nearer, Mr. and Mrs. Lyons paused, letting Daniel come forward alone.

He looked different. Better. Handsome. His hair was clean cut, shorter than she remembered with a cropped top and tapered sideburns. His face was fuller, and unlike the last time she saw him, it had a healthy glow about it. His eyes devoured her, and as she gazed back, her insides suddenly tingled, evoking the same feeling she'd had when she first met him in college.

"Hello, Colleen."

"It's C.B. now," she said caustically.

He looked as if he didn't comprehend her taunt. It didn't matter. As she measured him, she squared her shoulders and lifted her chin, hoping to somehow mask her apprehension.

"Thanks for letting me see Scotty." His voice cracked as if he too was nervous.

"I was told I had to let you see him."

His eyes lowered. "Yes, I know."

"Well, here he is. Here's my son." C.B. knelt beside Scotty who was staring up at his father. "Scotty, that's your daddy. It's okay to go with him to look at the fish."

Daniel knelt too and grasped Scotty's shoulders, pulling him into a hug. There were tears in Daniel's eyes. C.B. didn't want to see the tears. She didn't want to feel pangs of sorrow and regret.

As she rose to her feet, Daniel said, "Hi, Buddy. Remember me?"

Turning away from the reunion, C.B. suppressed the emotions that shifted through her heart. Her former in-laws approached with uncertain smiles on their faces.

"Scotty likes to look at the fish in the pond," C.B. told them. "It's okay if you want to walk around with him. If you buy the fish food, he likes to throw it into the water for the fish."

"Thanks for doing this, Colleen," Mrs. Lyons said holding back tears. "We've missed Scotty so much,"

C.B. stiffened. Why was she feeling guilt when the whole situation was not her fault? "We've been taking good care of him," she answered. "You didn't need to worry."

Her answer was rude. Unkind. She couldn't help it. C.B. backed away. She didn't want to have contact with these people. They were part of a previous life. That life had ended. Daniel had seen to that with his lies and betrayal.

As Daniel and his parents took Scotty around the pond, C.B. retreated to a picnic table near the swings. It was Tuesday, a workday and a school day, so the park was nearly empty. Sitting on the top of the picnic table with her feet on the bench seat, she had a good view of the family strolling around the ponds. They walked slowly, holding Scotty's hand. Once the little boy broke free and scampered to the water's edge. Daniel rushed forward and caught his hand again.

In another life, she would have watched the scene with a heart full of love and joy. Now all she felt was sadness. Shutting her eyes to close off the images of the idyllic family in the distance, C.B. longed for Jamie. The yearning was unexpected.

"I'm here if you need me," he'd said. And she needed him now.

Jamie would understand her anger and uncertainty. He would accept her for herself, not expecting her to be anything more. She sensed that about him. In the short time she'd known him, he'd never asked her to be anything more than the woman she wanted to be.

C.B. sat quietly a minute, breathing deeply of the spring air, letting the sun bathe her face, and willing a peace to descend upon her. In a nearby tree, a cardinal shrilled its "birdie, birdie, birdie" song. Wind stirred her hair and smoothed her brow.

When she opened her eyes again, that moment of serenity was gone. She took another deep breath watching Daniel approach the picnic table alone. His parents guided Scotty on another walk around the fishpond.

Standing in front of her, Daniel searched her face. He didn't say a word for a full minute, as if he was measuring her to gauge her reaction. Gone was the cocky assuredness he had once worn. In its place, Daniel seemed a shell of himself—of the man she had once loved.

"May I?" He nodded at the empty spot beside her on the table-top. "I need to talk to you."

C.B. shrugged. Might as well get this over. Then she could go home and back to work for Jamie.

Daniel climbed up and sat beside her. His shoulder brushed hers. He fisted his hands, rested his elbows on his knees and leaned forward so he didn't have to look at her.

"I've finished my rehab, Colleen," he said softly.

"I heard." She didn't want to make talking any easier for him.

"I've made it right with the law."

Anger roiled through her. "I'm sure your father helped."

Daniel swallowed. "He was there. And my mother."

But I wasn't. She heard his indictment.

"I've given up med school."

Right. You flunked out. C.B. kept her thoughts to herself.

Daniel sat back and turned to her. "I've had a lot of therapy. Getting clean was the hardest thing I've ever done. Learning the underlying cause of my addiction was painful."

She couldn't meet his eyes. Instead, C.B. focused on her son scampering along the path with his grandparents.

"I need to tell you this, Colleen. I need you to understand," Daniel pleaded.

"I'm listening." Her response was flat.

"You're not making this easy."

"Do you think my life has been a piece of cake?" She turned on him, furious. "Now you're back, and I can't keep you away from my son."

"I have my rights."

"You forfeited your rights that night when you and that bitch hit my car."

Daniel pulled himself up, sitting up straighter, as if trying to control his anger. His jaw clenched then he took several cleansing breaths. "My father said talking to you wouldn't be easy."

"Right." C.B. looked away, finding it difficult to breathe.

He touched her arm. "I've made many mistakes. I'm trying to make amends."

C.B. recoiled and glared at him. He removed his hand and turned away, resting his elbows once more on his knees and talking to the ground in a monotone voice.

"Through counseling I learned I was trying to live up to the expectations of my family. My father was a doctor. I had to become a doctor. When I flunked out of school, I couldn't tell anyone. They would have been disappointed in me. I started drinking. Drugs." He paused and swallowed hard. "I lost my way."

Daniel's explanation was more of an accusation in C.B.'s ears. He didn't say it. But she heard it. If she had been a better wife, not focused on being a mother, she could have prevented his downward spiral. That was unfair. A travesty. C.B. bit her lip in anger and remained quiet.

How ironic. The woman she'd been back then would have not been much help to him because she had relied on Daniel to be the rock, the steady and dependable force in her life that made everything better.

Surprised by her sudden self-awareness, C.B. clasped her hands on her lap and fought the quiver of her chin. She was not to blame in this, but maybe her reliance on Daniel, her expectations of him had contributed to his collapse.

"I've got my life back together," Daniel said. "I'm going to nursing school in the fall. Male nurses are in demand. I think I can do it. I want to help people, like people have helped me."

"That's nice."

He sat up and looked at her again. His eyes were alert and his jaw set. "I didn't get the chance to fight for you, Colleen, to fight for our family. By the time I'd come out of my stupor, you'd divorced me and moved on."

Moved on? Had she moved on? "I have an experienced lawyer in my family," she said by way of reaction.

"Yes, I know. Your father."

Daniel inhaled deeply through his nose and then exhaled through his mouth. He stood up in front of her, planting his feet in a wide stance. They were eye-to-eye.

"I intend to fight for you now, Colleen."

"C.B.," she said. "I'm C.B. now."

He grimaced, but continued. "I love you. I want you to come back to me. I want us to start over. I want us to be a family again."

Her mind raced, searching for answers. She found it hard to speak. She didn't know how to respond. What to say?

"Will you think about it, C.B.?" Daniel's eyes were wet. "Will you think about us being a family again?"

"Yes." Her answer was faint, the word lifting in the wind and winging away.

"Oh, God!" Daniel caught her hands, squeezing them. "That is all I can ask for. I still love you. I made a terrible mistake, but we can make it right again. For Scotty's sake, we can be a family again."

Unable to completely fill her lungs, C.B. looked down at their clasped hands and fought back tears.

CHAPTER FOURTEEN

Something dramatic had happened during C.B.'s morning visit with Daniel. Jamie knew it as certainly as he knew his own mind. When she came to work at two o'clock, she went back to her desk in the sunroom, hardly speaking. She wouldn't open up. Wouldn't look him in the eye. What had happened? Why was she shutting him out?

When she didn't leave at three, Jamie walked into the sunroom with a glass of iced tea. "You're not leaving?"

She looked up at him as if embarrassed and accepted the tea. "Thanks." She looked back at her keyboard. "My mom is watching Scotty again. I told her I wanted to catch up on my work."

"If you need to go home, I'll understand."

"No, I'm almost finished retyping this old galley. I want to finish it for you."

"Okay, I'll let you get back to work then," Jamie said. He hesitated, hoping she'd say more. When she didn't, he made small talk. "I really need to make progress on that new manuscript. It's not going well." He'd been stuck for days and his deadline loomed like an ugly cloud over his head.

C.B. didn't respond. He surveyed her pensive expression, her avoidance of direct eye contact. All he wanted to do was seize her and give her a shake, make her tell him what happened. But more than that, he yearned to pull her into his arms and love her again. Not simply to make love, but to love her—to show her how much he'd come to care for her.

He didn't do either. With a sigh, he turned and left the sunroom, dodging the issue as much as she had evaded him.

It was five o'clock when C.B. joined him in his office. Jamie looked up from his lined notebook paper. Crumpled wads of paper were scattered on the table and had fallen to the floor. He hadn't written a word worth keeping.

Studying him, her eyes brimming with misery, C.B. stood a moment in silence. His gaze raked her as the discomfort between them grew. What could he say to her? What had happened between them since last night?

She cleared her throat. "I've finished typing *The Scottish Captive Bride*," she said. "The file is in the computer. Do you want me to make a copy of it or something?"

Jamie pushed his chair back, trying to ignore the tightness in his chest. He tried to sound as if this was a normal conversation. "I will send the file to my copyreader. After she's finished, her husband will format it into an e-book. I'll soon have the old book self-published as Madison Mallory. Thanks for your help."

Publishing his mother's old books electronically had been such a big goal, one he hoped would bring him more income, but now it seemed secondary. His only concern was the woman standing beside his desk staring at him as if she'd lost her best friend.

"C.B., what is it?" Would she talk to him? He desperately hoped she'd confide in him.

"Uh. Daniel wants me back." Her voice trailed off.

He jumped to his feet. "What?"

"I don't know how to find the right words to tell you this." She touched her lips with her fingers and glanced behind him as if seeking the words she needed.

Jamie felt an uncontrollable flush of heat wash over his body. He tingled all over. Snatching her hand, he drew her down the hall and into the sunroom where he coaxed her to sit on the blue sofa. He sat down beside her and grasped her hand.

"Take your time," he said. "Tell me everything."

"Daniel said he was sorry. That he wants to fight for me now he's clean. That he wants us to be a family again."

C.B. had longed for a forever family. With Daniel in the picture again, Jamie assumed the worst-case scenario.

"What are you going to do?"

She turned to him, searching his face. "I don't know."

He wanted to say something—to declare himself, his love, his intentions. But what were they? Did he really want more from his relationship with C.B. than a quickie here, a night there? He'd told her he didn't care about the future, but now he did—desperately. Yet, she had warned him it wouldn't work because of Scotty. How could he expect her to be in a relationship with him when she had a small son to consider?

"Maybe it's best if you think about what Daniel said," he whispered, giving her his permission.

"I don't know." She looked confused. "I don't know what to do."

"He hurt you badly."

"But he says he's sorry." C.B. took a deep breath. Her eyes clouded, going distant as if she sought her answer elsewhere, not with him.

Jamie squeezed her hand. "You should take your time, but you shouldn't discount what he says. You said you wanted a family. Maybe going back to Daniel will restore your family and give you what you really want."

Her head slightly shook. "Are you sure?"

"Makes sense to me." Releasing her, giving her consent to go back to Daniel, was the hardest thing Jamie had done in his life.

She nodded then straightened her shoulders. "If I'm going to do this—consider Daniel's offer—I can't work for you any longer, Jamie."

He hadn't counted on that. "What?"

Her eyes welled with tears. "It will be too hard to see you if I'm going to go back to Daniel." She shook her head. "It isn't fair to you."

"I understand." But did he?

What had he done? Given up the most precious person to ever come into his life? His shoulders sagged with resignation. He couldn't believe it.

C.B. stood, and he came to his feet. God, this couldn't be happening.

"It's been great, Jamie."

"Yes." His voice cracked.

"You take care of yourself, okay?"

"You too, C.B."

He followed her to the front door and unlocked it. Should he grab her? Not let her go? Panic rose in his throat but he remained unmoving as if paralyzed.

"I don't regret a thing," she told him and then turned and went out the door.

He watched her go across the street. "I don't regret anything either," he said, but it was to himself.

Alone once more, Jamie shut the door and turned out the lights.

"You did what?" Kelly asked, fearing that the rise in her voice would scare Scotty.

When C.B. had called to say she'd be late, Kelly had gone

ahead and fixed supper for her grandson. Now Scotty sat at her kitchen table, his back to them and a plate of spaghetti and fresh apple slices in front of him.

"I quit my job," C.B. said and looked away. She couldn't meet her mother's eyes.

"Because you took Scotty to see his father?" Kelly didn't get the connection. "It doesn't make sense."

"Because Daniel wants us to get back together." C.B. sat down at the table and offered Scotty his glass of milk. "And I'm considering it."

"You are what?" Had her daughter lost her mind?

"If Daniel and I get back together, then it will be good for Scotty."

"But what about you?"

"What about me?"

"What do you want for yourself? If you're happy, your son will be happy," Kelly said. "It's as simple as that." Could C.B. actually consider going back to the man who'd broke her heart?

"We'd be a family again," C.B. said in a small voice.

"There are many kinds of families. I like to think you and I and Aunt Bess had a pretty good family. You never wanted for anything. You turned out just fine."

"Did I, Mom?"

Calm down, Kelly told herself. She didn't want to damage her relationship with C.B. but the girl was talking foolishness.

"Well, I think you turned out fine. You've been a great mother to Scotty, especially these last few months. No one could ask for a better mom. And personally, you've pulled yourself together. I don't see why you'd want to go back to that man."

Daniel had always held a strong influence over C.B., controlling her almost too much. Frankly, Kelly was glad for their divorce. She had her daughter back, not the doormat she'd been when married to Daniel.

"Because we'd be a family again," C.B. said in a plaintive voice.

"I hope you think this through."

C.B. picked up Scotty's dishes and carried them to the kitchen sink. "I plan to, Mom," she said. "This is my life. I'll live it my way."

"No one said you shouldn't," Kelly snapped back, annoyed. "I just don't want you to make that mistake again."

"Come on, Scotty." C.B. wiped her son's hands and face with a wet rag. "We've got to go home."

As Kelly saw her daughter and grandson to the door, C.B. got off a parting shot. "It's my mistake to make now, isn't it?"

"Of course it is, honey."

"I'll be okay, Mom. Don't worry about me."

Kelly laughed a scornful laugh. "You're a mother. You know that isn't possible for a mother."

"Well, at least try for the first time in your life," C.B. said in a huff and hurried Scotty out to her car.

"I still don't understand why you quit your job," Kelly called after them.

As she shut the door, the implications of that rash action hit Kelly full force. Something had gone on between James Madison and her daughter. Why else would she give up her job? And be in such a hurry to rush back into Daniel's arms?

CHAPTER FIFTEEN

Two weeks later

Life without work was miserable. Or maybe it was life without Jamie. C.B. understood she was like an addict and needed to go "cold turkey," or making another change in her life would not work. That's how she'd survived Daniel's betrayal and the divorce. Cold turkey. That's how she planned to survive getting over Jamie.

But the reunion with Daniel remained in limbo as well. Her ex's second visitation wasn't scheduled until tomorrow. C.B. was not going to run straight into his arms. He'd have to work to win her back.

"I wish your job across the street had worked out," Bekah commented while they made breakfast casseroles to freeze for busy mornings at the B&B.

Scotty played on the floor nearby. He had a new wooden train set that kept him busy for hours. Spending more time with Scotty was a happy by-product of quitting her job.

"Why?" C.B. replied. She was defensive about the whole episode with Jamie. "I have more time to help you."

"I'm grateful for the help, but I don't like to see you moping around."

"I'm not moping around."

"You could have fooled me."

Bekah was right. It was just that she didn't like uncertainty. When the reality of Daniel and his costume-clad companion had set in, she'd had direction. Divorce was a perfectly obvious solution to his betrayal. Today her situation had changed. Daniel was back declaring his love. And Jamie remained secluded across the street with his unwritten manuscript and the care of his mother on his mind. C.B. felt pulled both ways. There was no obvious path for her to take.

Drawing a hot casserole from the oven, C.B. reprimanded herself for her wishful thinking. She placed the hot dish on a cooling rack and removed the two oven mitts from her hands. How in her right mind could she consider Jamie as an alternative? The man was nothing more than her employer—part-time at that. Sure, she'd let herself become drawn into a quickie affair. No, more like a series of one-night-stands. Jamie had not once disclosed any kind of long-term intentions. In fact, he'd been silent on the subject. He'd even understood when she told him about Daniel and suggested she go back to her ex-husband.

Fresh pain ambushed her. C.B. bit her lip and turned from the casserole preparations to gaze fondly at her son. Watching him, so innocent, so ready for life, she knew her path was clear. She must make herself go back to Daniel.

But why would it be so hard? She didn't love Jamie, did she? And he certainly didn't love her. She'd practically begged him to proclaim his love when she saw him for the last time. He hadn't. She'd forced herself to leave. That was all there was to it. Cold turkey.

"C.B., can you get the door?" Bekah asked.

"What?"

"Someone's at the front door."

"Oh, right."

She'd been so intent on her problems she'd failed to hear the doorbell chime. Wiping her hands on a towel, C.B. left the newly remodeled kitchen and crossed the wooden living room floor. Not bothering to check before she opened the front door, she flung it open.

"Good morning, C.B."

Jamie.

Simply standing on the porch, he seemed to suck the oxygen from the air. C.B. fought to breathe. In the cool light of mid-morning, he looked horrible—as if he hadn't slept. His hair was disheveled, his face unshaven. Dark circles rimmed his eyes. His white T-shirt rumpled. It looked as if he'd thrown it and his jeans on and crammed his feet into his shoes to walk across the street.

The two of them surveyed each other for an emotional moment as if at loss for words.

"I'm sorry to bother you, C.B., but I need your help again." He carried a laptop and on top of it balanced a cardboard box.

She thrilled to the rich timber of his voice. She loved his voice. She was also happy to see him but shoved down any overt reaction, controlling her features and her own tone.

"Can we talk?"

C.B. came out onto the porch, shutting the door behind her. She could talk to him sitting on the porch swing, but it held too many memories. She simply turned to face him.

"What do you want?"

He regarded her, his eyes softening with longing. Or did she read them right? She had a miserable track record with men, always wishing for more than they could give. C.B. chided herself for interpreting what was not there.

"I've finished *My Highland Bride*," he said and extended his hands.

Her gaze dropped to the box and laptop. So, he'd finished his new manuscript. The one he'd struggled with all the time she worked for him.

Looking up, she gave him a tight smile of concession. "Congratulations."

He glanced away, drew a breath, and turned back to her. "You know I'm under strict deadline."

She nodded. Could she guess what was coming?

"You know I can't type."

C.B. reached out to him. "I'll type it."

"Will you, C.B.? That will be wonderful."

Taking the load from him, she hugged the box and laptop close to her chest. "But I won't do it at your house."

"That's why I brought the laptop," he said. "I thought you could type it over here."

She nodded again. Her mouth was dry and her body tense. He smiled at her, a genuine smile that seemed to come from his heart then looked away.

"I've rewritten some of the scenes and finished the last one hundred pages. I rewrote everything, starting from the beginning, so you can read it easier. Start fresh if you want." He surveyed her once more, an amused smile tugging at the corner of his lips. "If you can read my handwriting."

"I can read it." Her reply was curt. In her heart, though, C.B. cried for the strangers they had so suddenly become.

"Great." Jamie took a step back seeming uncomfortable. "I hated to ask you."

"I don't mind."

He nodded and took another step back. "Great. How's it going?"

"Fine."

His lips tensed into a line as if struggling to find words. "I've burned a lot of midnight oil to get this done," he said.

"I figured as much."

He smiled at her again. "You understand why it's so important to me?"

"I understand. I'll work on it and get it back to you soon."

"Thank you, C.B."

"No problem."

Jamie backed another step, smiled once more, and dropped his eyes. Then he turned and left the porch. She stared after him, angry with herself for not being able to think of a single thing to say. Maybe it was because she had no clue what she wanted to say.

No clue but the regret that filled her aching heart.

CHAPTER SIXTEEN

No wonder Jamie looked like hell when C.B. saw him—his manuscript was long. He'd finished it then rewritten it by hand from the start. Two hundred and forty typed pages, eight-five thousand or so words, translated to a lot of handwritten pages. She started typing the manuscript that day during Scotty's nap. From the beginning, she recognized more passion in the story as if a light had turned on in Jamie's brain that enabled him to write from the depths of his soul.

Could she have been that light? She'd never know, she guessed. Jamie remained as reticent and reclusive as the day she first met him.

Later that afternoon before dinner, C.B.'s grandmother showed up at the B&B with a gift for Scotty.

"I found these wooden train pieces at a yard sale," Grace Baron Scott told her granddaughter. "These aren't the expensive cartoon-character ones, but the seller told me these engines and train cars fit with those sets as well."

"Scotty," C.B. called to her son. They were upstairs in their carriage-house apartment, and the little boy came dashing out of his room. "Look at what Gran brought you."

The boy seemed enthralled by the set. "Thanks," he said shyly.

"Give Gran a hug," C.B. instructed.

Scotty encircled Gran's waist with his little arms. "I love you, Buddy," Gran said.

Once Scott disappeared into his room with his new toys, C.B. offered to make her grandmother a glass of iced tea.

"That's fine," Grace said. "Your mother tells me I'm needed to make an intervention."

"Oh, oh, here it comes." C.B. and her mother had not parted under the best of terms. Because she and Gran had always been close, it looked like Kelly had sent her mother over to try to persuade C.B. out of going back to Daniel.

Gran moved a stuffed lamb from the sofa and sat down as C.B. brought the frosty glass of sweetened tea. "Thank you, dear."

C.B. joined her on the sofa. "Why is it my mother never changes?" There was levity in her voice. She knew her mother well.

"You're a mother," Grace replied. "You know the mother-bear syndrome."

"All too well, I'm afraid."

The older woman took a sip of tea. "You're precious to your mother, C.B. She only wants what's best for you."

"Don't you think I know that? But she's not one to criticize. Her fear of speaking up cost me a childhood with my father."

Grace inclined her head in acknowledgement. "Everyone makes mistakes."

"And I've certainly made mine," C.B. admitted. "Don't worry. I haven't committed to anything yet. I'm leaving my options open."

Grace studied the drink in her hands as if weighing what she wanted to say next. "Your mother thinks you had more feelings for Mr. Madison than you'll confess."

Laughing aloud, C.B. fought a twinge of anger and annoyance. "You see Mom can't bring herself to say that to my face, so she sends you."

"I suppose peacemaking is part of my duty as family matriarch," Grace said with a shrug.

C.B. exhaled a big breath. "Well, if I've learned one thing, it's that unrequited love sucks. I don't intend to let myself fall victim to it ever again."

Grace smiled as if congratulating herself. "That's my girl."

"So you can tell Mom to rest easy."

"I'll do that. Can I give you some advice?"

C.B. sat back and returned the smile. Gran was so wonderfully direct. "Can I stop you?"

"No." Grace surveyed her with a look of love. "I learned through my years of experience to forgive. Your grandfather. Myself. You need to forgive Daniel, honey. And forgive yourself too. Then move on with your life."

"It's hard," C.B. said, looking away.

"Especially when you find yourself in love again?"

C.B.'s head jerked around, and she stared at her grandmother whose shrewd question was like a slap to C.B.'s face. She'd denied loving Jamie. Yet, here was her grandmother putting her finger precisely on C.B.'s problem.

"How do I move on with my life, Gran?" she asked in a small voice. "I know the pitfalls of loving someone too much, of not having that love returned. How can I move on with my life when Jamie doesn't want me?"

"Simple." Grace placed her glass on a side-table coaster. "I wish I'd had someone to give me this advice when I was young."

C.B. took a deep breath and gave her grandmother a slight smile. "Okay, let me have it."

"Go it alone. Create your life without a man." Grace paused. "Like your mother did. Like Bekah."

"But you and Mom are happily married," C.B. protested.

Grace shook her head. "It took years. I was too dependent on your grandfather. It wasn't healthy. Your mother reacted by going the other way and not marrying when she found herself pregnant. I hope you learn from our mistakes."

C.B. sat quietly a moment, her mind racing in a thousand different directions. "I know you're right, Gran," she finally conceded. "It's just hard."

"Life is hard," Grace said. "I know it's cliché, but that is how we learn" She stood up. "Come on and give me a hug."

C.B. jumped to her feet and hugged her grandmother. She smelled of vanilla and shampoo. She seemed frailer than C.B. remembered. However, Gran remained her rock. Dependable. Loving.

"Some of us take longer to learn the hard lessons than others," Grace whispered. "Don't you be like your mother and me."

"I'll try, Gran. I really will."

HER GRANDMOTHER'S visit left C.B. sad and disheartened. After a quick supper, C.B. took Scotty to the park so she could clear her head. Watching her son scramble up and down the wooden play set, she railed silently at her grandmother's words. Life shouldn't be hard. It should be simple and straightforward like life was with Daniel before the giant debacle. Life was so much easier then. She was happy. Scotty was secure. She had a family.

But she had lived a lie. And she wasn't willing to do that again.

Coming to terms with that reality was in effect freeing. C.B. took a cleansing breath of the spring air and returned to her second-floor apartment. When Scotty went to bed at eight o'clock, she began typing Jamie's manuscript. She wanted to get it off her plate. She wanted to move on.

Trouble reared its ugly head at chapter three. The writing pulled her in. It was so much better. Deeper. The characters were so real—their dialogue so compelling and unique to each character. As she typed, C.B. visualized the setting and the emotions. She related to what was taking place.

"Oh, my gosh, Jamie. What have you done?" she whispered to herself.

The love scene she'd initially typed had been strengthened. There were also three more of them, the hero knight making love to his beloved. However, once Jamie changed point of view to the heroine, those love scenes remained static. They needed genuine emotion. Maybe it was something Jamie couldn't give in a female perspective.

This was fantasy, after all, but his work needed help. Immersed in the story as she typed, C.B. decided to play with her imagination and give Jamie the help he needed. It was dark outside. She stood up and stretched, then went to her bedroom window. She couldn't see Main Street or Jamie's house from the window because the B&B blocked the view. But she shut her eyes and envisaged it. She thought about her feelings when he had carried her upstairs. When they made love. Her emotions suddenly swept her away. She swayed as she stood at the window, feeling it, living it again in memory.

Then she sat back down at the laptop and typed her version of the heroine's point of view during the first love scene. The second. She dug deep into her psyche. Into her lust and desire. Into her love.

At three o'clock in the morning, C.B. finished typing the complete manuscript into the file on the laptop. It needed to be backed up so she wouldn't lose the document, so she emailed the file to Jamie. Luckily, after she'd started to work for him, he'd bought another computer, so he could receive email on something larger than his cell phone.

She was tired—exhausted physically and mentally. There was an underlying sadness to her fatigue. Pouring herself out into the words and actions of the fictitious heroine had drained her and made her long for a reality that mirrored the fantasy she had created. Did Jamie live in such a made-up world? Not quite real? Only dreams of what could be?

Yet the changes he'd composed felt so life-like C.B. wanted to believe in them. She yearned for them to be real. And that's when it hit her—like a slap to the head.

Jamie had written the love scenes about her.

CHAPTER SEVENTEEN

Jamie crawled out of bed at five a.m. He couldn't sleep. Hadn't been able to sleep for two weeks since C.B. left, and especially now that he'd given his precious manuscript to her. In his shorts and T-shirt, he plodded into the kitchen and made himself a cup of coffee. The dawn had not yet broken. Carrying his cup, he turned on the light to his office and stared at the mess of his so-called desk. It needed cleaning so he tossed trash, all while sipping his coffee and thinking.

His relationship with Julia had been ruined when he'd failed to express himself. How ironic was it that he had finally found a way to express his feelings? And in his romance novel, of all things. But it was too late, wasn't it? Too late for C.B. and him.

Finally, when all litter had been removed, Jamie sat down at his desk. The new computer monitor blinked back at him when he turned it on. He might as well get comfortable with the damn thing. He would need to learn to use the word processing program and stop using his absent-minded professor excuse to avoid it.

When he opened the email program, he was surprised to see

C.B.'s email. "I have finished typing the manuscript," the message read. "It's good."

Nothing more. The cryptic note disappointed him. He felt his chest ache under the weight of its sorrow.

Clicking on the file, his manuscript sprang to life in front of him. He scrolled through the text. It looked so much better typed. He'd be able to meet his deadline after all.

When he came to the first love scene, he read it word for word, huddling close to the monitor screen. Several pages later, he had switched points of view to the heroine's. He read those silently. Then he sat up straighter. That wasn't his text. Scrolling back, he read them again. He swallowed, closing his eyes. A chill darted through him.

C.B. had added to his love scene, writing words filled with tenderness and emotion.

BY ELEVEN O'CLOCK, Jamie had showered and changed into jeans and a gray sweater. His mood had lifted, causing him to be almost jovial. Damn! He had a chance. He simply needed to tell her how he felt—in person, not on paper. Had C.B. realized he described his feelings for her when his medieval knight hero declared his devotion to his ladylove? There was only one way to find out.

Jamie crossed the street under the pretext of retrieving his laptop, and was astonished when his doorbell ring was answered right away.

"Oh," C.B. said, a look of surprise on her face. "I thought you were Daniel."

"No." He suddenly found himself tongue tied. "I wanted to get my laptop back since you finished the manuscript last night."

"Oh, yes. Was it okay?"

"It was more than okay, C.B. It was wonderful." Did she understand what he meant?

"I'm glad you approve."

"I was wondering if I could talk to you about it."

She looked over his shoulder, appearing anxious. "I'm expecting Daniel any minute. To pick up Scotty."

Daniel. Anger jabbed him in the gut. It smacked of jealousy. He hated the thought of leaving without saying what he'd come to say.

"May I wait on the porch until you're available?" He inclined his head toward the swing.

For a moment they stood silent and unmoving. He read her indecision. Then a car pulled up in front of the house. Jamie didn't turn toward it. He held his ground, pleading to C.B. with his eyes.

"Yes," she said breathlessly. "Wait on the swing until Daniel takes Scotty."

He'd bought a reprieve. Jamie strode to the porch swing and sat down, moving it gently with his feet. The car, a Porsche, was filled with three people. A man and a woman sat in the front. A young man climbed out of the back seat and headed up the sidewalk. He glanced at Jamie and scowled.

"Who's that guy?" Daniel asked when C.B. brought Scotty to the door.

"My former boss," she told him.

"What's he doing here?"

C.B. pulled herself upright and frowned. "It's none of your business, Daniel."

"I want to know what he's doing around my son." Daniel caught Scotty by the hand when the little boy tried to hide behind his mother's back.

"He's *my* son, Daniel, and Scotty is not around him. Jamie has come to see me."

Her comment spurred Jamie to action. He stood and walked

toward the couple. "I've got business with C.B." he said and gave the man a challenging grin. "You don't mind, do you?"

"Frankly, I do."

Jamie cocked his head. Damn, he didn't like this guy. "I thought you two were divorced."

Daniel stood his ground. "We may be divorced, but I intend to change that soon."

"Are you so sure?" Jamie asked, contesting again. "I'm sure C.B. will have something to say about her change in circumstances."

"Who are you, anyway, buddy?" Daniel asked. He was angry.

"I'm simply a man who loves her and wants to marry her." Jamie turned toward C.B., taking in her mouth opened wide in shock. He smiled at her and said, "Truly."

"Wait a minute, bud!"

C.B. acted quickly, stepping between them. "You wait a minute, Daniel Lyons. Think of where you are. Think of Scotty. I don't want you two to fight."

Abashed, Daniel lowered his head. "Okay. You're right." He shot a look of hatred at Jamie. "I don't like him, Colleen, but he's not worth getting worked up about. Let's go, Scotty."

An older man had gotten out of the car and had started toward the porch as if he would join in the confrontation. When Daniel brought Scotty down the steps, the man caught Scotty into his arms, gave him a hug, and carried him to the car. Daniel buckled Scotty into his car seat. The Porsche pulled away from the curb.

Jamie turned back to C.B. The tension in her stance warned him all was not well. "That was pleasant," he said sarcastically.

"What do you mean, James Madison, barging into my family's affairs like you did?"

He scowled at the reprimand. "That man thinks he owns you."

"And what about you and that remark you made?"

"I wanted you to know the truth. How I feel about you."

C.B. inhaled a shuddering breath. "Wasn't that evident in your manuscript?"

"I didn't know if you'd understand," he said quietly, standing firm.

"I understood," she snapped. "All too well."

Breaking away from him, C.B. walked to the swing and plopped down on it. As if she couldn't remain still, she moved it with her feet. He joined her, pausing in front of her, looking down at her eyes filled with tears.

He bit back a curse. "I didn't mean to make you cry."

"What *did* you mean?"

"I wanted to declare my intentions. I love you, C.B. I want to marry you."

A bitter smile flashed across her face. "Isn't *that* interesting."

Jamie broke eye contact. This wasn't going right. Not as planned. Trouble was, he hadn't planned anything. He'd simply acted on impulse, on the knowledge she loved him too.

Or at least so he had hoped.

Jamie sat down beside her and added his weight to the swing. The swaying motion halted. Without asking, he placed his arm around her shoulders and pulled her close. The scent of her hair reminded him of their time together.

The chance he took paid off, and she wilted against him. "Oh, Jamie, why are things so complicated? So hard?"

"You think love is hard?"

"Yes. And life. Everything. Motherhood, marriage, relationships—they are all hard."

"I guess it's the way things are."

"I know."

He rocked her then, letting the movement of the swing sooth their shattered nerves. He finally whispered into her sweet-smelling hair, "I loved what you added to my love scenes."

She spoke softly. "They needed help."

"I think they were written from your heart."

He felt her head nod. "They were."

"I meant what I said in front of Daniel. I know you want to have a family, and I want to give that to you. I love you, C.B."

"I know that now, Jamie, and I love you too."

He wanted to jump for joy, sing the "Hallelujah Chorus," and march in a parade. Life was suddenly wonderful. If Colleen Baron Lyons loved him, all was perfect.

She tilted her head up and looked him in the eyes. He saw the love there, as well as the indecision. She ran a finger on the line over his mouth.

"The thing is," she said. "I'm not ready to marry you now. I've not had enough time to create my own life."

"But you were going to marry Daniel," he protested.

She shook her head. "No, silly Jamie. I told you I didn't know what I wanted to do. I wanted you to fight for me, but you didn't. You let me go. I really don't want to remarry Daniel."

"Truly?" He couldn't believe it. His relief was intense.

"Truly," she said.

He'd try anything. "What about a long engagement?"

She laughed at him. With him. It was a laugh filled with love and surrender. "I want to create my life, and I want you to be part of that creation. So, yes, James Madison, a long engagement will suit me just fine."

Jamie kissed her then, cupping her face in his hands, his lips hard and quick and demanding. "Promise me?" he murmured.

She made a soft sound of acquiescence. "I promise."

EPILOGUE

Twelve Months Later
Book Signing
Lexington, Kentucky

A huge banner of a medieval knight in full battle armor stood at the entrance to the bookstore. *My Highland Bride* read the caption. Beneath the title were the words "By James Madison writing as Madison Mallory."

C.B. snapped a picture of the banner with her cell phone. She was here to surprise Jamie. The last time she'd been signing the books for him, pretending to be Madison Mallory. As a mark of his newfound confidence in his writing ability and with his editor's agreement, Jamie now took credit for the books. After his mother passed six months earlier, he no longer required a guaranteed income. He could sink or swim under his own reputation.

But his newest book was doing well. Jamie had attributed the sales to C.B.'s influence. During the last year, they had collaborated on another historical romance. He had still not learned to type.

Smiling to herself, comfortable now in her own skin, C.B. wound her way through the bookshelves and displays until she spotted the table where Jamie signed books. There was a crowd. She joined the line, her paperback copy of the new book in hand.

Things had settled down with Daniel and his parents as well. Her ex saw Scotty every other weekend. Sometimes during the week he took their son to dinner. Moving to Lexington where he attended nursing school had made their lives easier.

A fan in front of C.B. turned and in a conspiratorial voice said, "Don't you just think he's the cutest thing?"

"Oh, yes," C.B. said breathlessly, amusement curling her toes.

"Don't you love his books? It's sad about his mother though. I loved the old Madison Mallory books."

"Yes, it's sad. But I think he does a good job."

"They're wonderful," the woman fan said, drooling.

When it was her turn at the table, C.B. shoved the book in front of Jamie. He didn't look up. "Whom do you want me to make it to?" he asked.

"You can make it to Colleen Baron," she said with a laugh.

He glanced up. "Hey, you."

Warmth rushed through C.B.'s body, and her heart exploded with happiness. They had an emotionally intimate relationship, one not just in the bedroom. They were friends first. Equals. She'd created her life with Jamie included in it.

"Hey, yourself."

"Thanks for coming," he said, "but I could have signed the book at home."

"I wanted to do it here, to see you signing without the nom de plume."

Jamie opened the front and flipped to the title page. His pen was poised for the autograph when he read what she had written there. *It's time. I'm ready. Will you marry me?*

Jamie pumped his fist. "Yes!" Then springing to his feet, he reached over the table and drew her into his arms.

She leaned toward him stretching as far as she could and whispered into his ear, "Promise kept."

The End

MORE ABOUT THE BLUEGRASS HOMECOMING SERIES

To my readers...

I wrote the novel *Secrets* a few years ago, choosing to explore a romance about a woman caught between the past and her desire to explore her future. I wanted to submit the manuscript to a traditional publisher, but was advised, at the time, this publisher did not like forty-year-old heroines. Since then, "seasoned" romance has come into wider acceptance.

After changing the setting of the story, *Secrets* became the second book in my new Bluegrass Homecoming series, a series that will let me again explore the themes of second chances in the Bluegrass of Kentucky.

To start my new series, I've written about the love story of baby boomers Howie and Grace. Their granddaughter C.B. takes center stage in the third book, *Nom de Plume*.

I foresee more books in the series, because there are many characters in *Secrets* begging to have their own stories.

Happy reading,
Jan

ABOUT THE AUTHOR

Whether it is the Bluegrass of Kentucky, the mountains of Montana, or Medieval England, Jan Scarbrough brings you home with romances from the heart.

Jan Scarbrough is the author of two popular Bluegrass series, writing heartwarming contemporary romances about home and family, single moms and children, and if the plot allows, about another passion—horses. Living in the horse country of Kentucky makes it easy for Jan to add small town, Southern charm to her books and the excitement of a Bluegrass horse race or a competitive horse show.

Leaving her contemporary voice behind, Jan has written paranormal gothic romances: Tangled Memories, a Romance Writers of America (RWA) Golden Heart finalist, and Timeless. Her medieval romance, My Lord Raven is a story of honor and betrayal.

A member of Novelist, Inc., Jan self-publishes her books with the help of her husband. She has published 25 romances.

Jan lives in Louisville, Kentucky, with two rescued dogs, one rescued cat, and a husband she rescued 21 years ago.

When she isn't writing, she loves to ride American Saddlebred horses, drive grandchildren to activities, and volunteer with Alley Cat Advocates. There is nothing she enjoys more than curling up with a good book.

Join Jan's mailing list at https://www.janscarbrough.com/ for news about new books and other possible appearances in your area. Follow Jan on Twitter @romancerider.

WANT MORE OF THE BLUEGRASS HOMECOMING SERIES?

Would marrying Howard be the trap Grace fears, or would it finally give her a kind of freedom she'd never imagined?

Prequel
The Bluegrass Homecoming
Book 1

Thursday Grief Support Group
First United Methodist Church

Heritage Springs, Kentucky

"I've buried two wives," the man said. "I miss them. I'm not good living alone."

Grace Baron pressed her lips into a tight line, and her gaze flitted from the only man in the circle to the three other widows. They'd all been left behind to cope, just as she had. They weren't doing well, it seemed, by the looks of them, especially a young woman sitting next to her crying and dabbing her eyes with a tissue. She couldn't stop the tears. Her grief consumed her.

Was there something wrong with her? Why didn't she miss her husband of almost forty years? In fact, in her heart of hearts, she was glad for the sudden freedom. She'd always been some-body's wife and mother, defined by those roles. All she wanted now was to live a little in the time left her.

There was only one problem—she didn't know *how* to live.

She didn't know herself—her wants, her likes. Being submissive to her husband in an old school way, she'd never explored the world. Herself. Her grief came more from regret, not sorrow. And guilt. She had a lot of that—from her mistakes as a young woman to those she'd made with her only daughter. And a big part of her was sad she'd never stood up for herself. Never had the courage, the courage she'd somehow given her daughter.

"Do you know how you're going to handle your grief, Howard?" June Hobson asked.

June was the volunteer who ran the support group and Grace's childhood friend, a friendship that had suffered during her marriage. The church didn't have a trained professional, but June had lost her husband almost fifteen years earlier. She'd seen this grief support group as her calling. Helping others, she'd said, had brought her out of her heartache. So, it had been natural for June to reach out to Grace when her husband died, draw her back to church, and into the group for support.

It had taken more than a year before Grace had felt comfortable enough to join. But here she was, her first day in the group—wide-eyed, cautious, and mouth shut.

"In my opinion, it's never too late to find true love," Howard answered. He was serious. His blue eyes stared pointedly at June. "I plan to marry again."

The young woman next to Grace gasped. "How can you? Isn't that disloyal to your wife's memory?"

"I cherish the memory of both my wives," he said, calmly pointing out he was not new to remarrying. "They both gave me love. One gave me a son. But they are gone now, and I am not."

It seemed so simple for this man, but it was an option Grace found awful.

"I will never marry again," Grace said in a quiet tone. All eyes turned to her.

"And why is that, Grace?" June asked.

"I don't trust love."

How could she? Not after what she'd gone through being married all those years to Lee Baron.

"But you love your daughter," June observed.

Grace lowered her eyes and stared at her hands. She hadn't made herself clear. The inability to communicate had been one of her problems during her marriage. She looked up at the members of the group. "Between a husband and wife," she clarified.

The room was silent. Only the quiet sobs of the woman sitting next to Grace broke the stillness.

"That's the saddest thing I've heard all day," Howard finally said in his deep baritone voice.

Grace lifted her gaze to meet his compassionate one. She knew this man. How could she not know the former mayor of Heritage Springs and a prominent town lawyer? They'd never personally met, never been in the same social circles, but Howard Scott was well known to everyone in the small community.

As they stared at each other, Grace became defensive. What right did he have to judge her? She'd lived her life the best she knew how. She'd been loyal, accepting the consequences of her actions. Pleasing her parents, her husband. In the end, she'd not pleased her daughter and lost her, but she'd made her choices for reasons she thought moral.

Raising her chin and tilting back her head, Grace refused to buckle under the man's scrutiny. She'd spent her life doing that. Never again. No, never again.

<u>Prequel: Bluegrass Homecoming, book 1</u>

WANT ANOTHER BLUEGRASS ROMANCE?

Sometimes a gamble pays off, especially when betting on love...

Betting on Love

Fourth Street Live!
Downtown, Louisville, Kentucky

They were arguing again. The noise in the Fourth Street Live! nightclub practically drowned out all thought, let alone conversation, but Sarah Colby could hear well enough to know her friends Kate and Tracy were quarrelling about her.

"You can't know a man by just one kiss," Kate said in a shrill voice, swiveling her barstool back and forth and stabbing a straw in and out of a frothy piña colada.

"Lighten up," Tracy chided. "Don't say that to Sarah. She believes it and she's finally ready to look for her prince."

"By kissing men?"

Stifling a sigh, Sarah looked around. The place was packed. With the Kentucky Derby only three weeks away, people were partying long before the day of the fabled race.

Sarah lifted her wine glass and studied her barhopping companions—Tracy, single but looking, and Kate, divorced and not looking. They had been her sorority sisters at the University of Kentucky and her best friends in the whole wide world.

"You know the fairy tale about the frog prince," Tracy said.

"Men are disgusting toads," Kate announced. "Don't be stupid. Kissing a man won't turn a toad into Prince Charming."

Tracy was right. Sarah didn't appreciate Kate's negative remarks. It wasn't the encouragement she needed, when she'd decided to go for it again.

Once she had believed in fairy tales. As a little girl, Sarah had lain awake at night dreaming of her prince. She had imagined him walking toward her with a warm smile on his lips and a tender look in his eyes. Tall. Dark. He would put his arms around her and kiss her. Slow and easy. The image always faded with the kiss. But Sarah knew, just by that one kiss, he was the man she would marry.

After all, that's how it had happened with her mom and dad. They'd met on New Year's Eve at a bar where guys were kissing girls at midnight. Her mom had told her she'd known she would marry her father from that very first kiss as "Auld Lang Syne" played and balloons dropped from the ceiling.

Sarah didn't believe in fairy tales now, but she had believed in her mother. Wasn't it normal to want to be cherished? To love and be loved? Who was to say one fateful kiss couldn't tell a woman the truth about a man?

At twenty-four, Sarah realized it was now time to get serious. She had dated more than her share of frat boys in college, but when their kisses failed to ignite a spark, she'd dropped them all without a second chance. Why waste her time with just one of them only to end up disappointed in the end?

Here at the nightclub, the place was crawling with men. Why not sample a few of them? Maybe she'd get lucky. It only took one kiss, after all.

"I doubt anything I say will stop Sarah from making a fool of herself," Kate said shaking her head. "Women do stupid things where men are concerned. Look at me."

"We're not here for one of your pity-parties," Tracy replied. "We want to help Sarah find her one true love."

"By kissing strange men?" Kate's voice dripped with sarcasm.

Sarah shifted uncomfortably on the stool and tugged down the skimpy, black dress that hiked up her thigh. "Quiet, both of you. We're here for two good reasons. We're celebrating the anniversary of Kate's divorce."

Tracy said brightly, "And you're here to find Prince Charming by kissing a few frogs."

"Toads," Kate amended under her breath.

Tracy wagged a finger at Kate. "You didn't think David was a toad when you married him."

"Well, the jerk fooled me. The man I thought was Prince Charming morphed into a toad as soon as the wedding ring was on my finger." Kate slurped down the rest of her piña colada and stared sadly at them.

Sarah's chest tightened. Her romantic heart knew there was a guy somewhere just for her. She didn't want to believe all men were like Kate's ex. And her practical side knew the way to find him.

Sarah leaned forward on her barstool. "Look, Kate, it's very simple. To make sure you've found the right man, you need a point of reference. You need a baseline. That's why you have to kiss a lot of men. My mom always guaranteed this method works to find the right one."

"There are *no* guarantees," Kate grumbled into her empty glass.

"We know that." Tracy waved Kate's objection away. "We're being proactive here. Sarah has a plan."

"And how many toads have you kissed?" Kate challenged Tracy, unable to let go of the topic.

Tracy frowned, her normal optimistic smile fading. She shook her head slightly, then spoke honestly, "Too many, I'm afraid."

"And you haven't found Mr. Right," Kate pointed out.

"You don't have to remind me."

"So, it's a stupid idea."

Sarah ignored Kate and fixed her attention on Tracy. "Where do you think I should start?"

"Let's look for suitable candidates." Tracy swiveled around and surveyed the whole nightclub. "Check out that guy over there hitting on the blonde."

Sarah studied the man in low-rider jeans and a bicep-baring tank top. That guy wasn't her type. She grimaced. "Looks coarse to me, but I'll give him a try. Gotta start somewhere."

Kate wrinkled her nose. "By the looks of that guy, I *guarantee* he'll be glad to let you try."

Tracy swiveled around. "Or there's that babe magnet sitting beside you."

Sarah turned and eyed the man hunched over his drink. He seemed oblivious to the clamor around him, but she liked his clean-cut, mature good looks.

She sipped her wine. Those were her options. If her aunt had her way, she wouldn't be going back to graduate school this summer. A food critic, Aunt Amelia wanted Sarah to do research for the regional cookbook she was writing. Not much chance of meeting Prince Charming if she was stuck in a dusty library or behind a laptop working for her aunt.

Besides, she had come dressed tonight for the occasion, prepared to get on with the job of finding a man to marry.

She was still a freakin' virgin, for crying out loud. It was now or never.

Sarah drew a deep breath and released it. Then eyeing the crude guy who'd just been dumped by the blonde, she said to her friends, "Okay, ladies. Time to pucker up. Time to kiss a toad and see what happens."

THE BLUEGRASS REUNION SERIES RETURNS!

Kentucky Woman

What is Jack willing to do to win the heart of this spirited Kentucky woman?

Kentucky Blue Bloods

When Kentucky blue blood tangles with British blue blood, are they willing to take a gamble on love?

Kentucky Bride / Kentucky Heat

Two novellas in one book

How far is Cam willing to go for his business? Can he turn a skittish Kentucky horse trainer into his Kentucky bride?

<>

Is Reggie crazy to think she can convince Hank he's more than just his daddy's name and fortune, without getting tangled up in his alluring Kentucky heat?

Kentucky Flame

Is there enough of an ember in the ashes of their past to reignite the flames of love?

Kentucky Groom

Can a marriage of convenience prove that a California millionaire can be the perfect Kentucky groom?

Kentucky Cowboy

Will Mandy take a second chance with her Kentucky cowboy and risk her heart this time?

Kentucky Rain

Carrying a torch is ridiculous. There's no time like the present to move on. But does Scott really want to?

Contemporary romances about second chances set in the Bluegrass of Kentucky that can be read as standalone novels with happily ever after endings and no cliffhangers.

THANK YOU!

For purchasing this book from
Saddle Horse Press